PAC NORTH
«« WOLVES »»

BOYS OF
RICHLAND
x x x

THE
REPLAY

USA TODAY BESTSELLING AUTHOR
DANIELA ROMERO

before you begin...

This story is so incredibly special to me. What Gabriel and
Cecilia go through... it's a lot.
If you're new to my Boys of Richland series, while not required,
I recommend you start with The Savage so you can see what it
all begins. If you've read it already, welcome back. I hope you
enjoy this next chapter in Gabriel and Cecilia's story.

xx Daniela

please read responsibly

The Striker is recommended for mature readers 17+
If you don't have any triggers, turn the page and enjoy.
If you do, check out the list below and make sure this book is a
good fit for you!

If Gabriel & Cecilia's story gets to be too much, you can put the
book down, take a break, or walk away.

The Replay much like other books of mine deals with social
issues and real-world problems. Some of your views may differ
from those of my characters and that is entirely okay. But please
don't message me to tell me "I'm wrong" about a particular
social issue. I'm not here to convince you one way or the other.
Your opinions are your own.

The Replay is not a standalone novel.
Gabriel and Cecilia's story begins with
The Savage and continues here in The Striker.
It will conclude here in The Replay.

one

GABRIEL

MY FRUSTRATION MOUNTS with each second that passes. "What do you mean, you won't go out and look for her?" I demand, my voice echoing through the sterile lobby of the Richland Police Department.

The asshole behind the counter doesn't seem to understand the severity of the situation right now.

My girl is missing.

She didn't wander off. She's not hanging out with friends and ignoring her phone.

She. Is. Missing.

I've searched all over campus. The pool. The Wolf Den. The soccer field. Julio spoke to Adriana. She's not with her. Atticus and Deacon checked all the common spaces at PacNorth U and came up empty-handed. We've all taken turns calling her phone. And still, nothing.

I'm spiraling here and running out of places to look.

Felix checked in with Cecilia's parents right before we came to the station. She hadn't gone home yet, either.

Dread settles low in my gut.

I have to find her.

"Sir, it's been less than twenty-four hours since your friend was last—"

I slam my fist down on the counter, the sound reverberating through the room. "He's out," I snarl at the rent-a-cop behind the desk. "The asshole who tried to kill her only a few weeks ago is out there." I wave my arm wildly toward the entrance. "And on the day he's released, Cecilia's nowhere to be found. That doesn't strike you as suspicious? This isn't a coincidence. He has her. Holt—"

The officer heaves a long-suffering sigh. "Look, kid, as I've already mentioned, Mr. Holt's whereabouts have been determined. He's under strict house arrest until his trial—"

"Then he has her in his home," I interject. "He probably has her chained to the floor in some creepy fucker dungeon in that mansion he calls a house. Did you check? Like, with your eyes?" He rests his hand on his holster, and I force myself to take a breath. Fuck. This asshole is going to kick me out of here if I don't calm down. Or worse, arrest me for making a scene. And then where would I be?

With more restraint than I realize I'm capable of, I lower my voice and grind out, "Do you know for a fact he's home and that she isn't in there with him?"

The officer huffs, his patience running on fumes. "Sir—"

Goddammit! It's that fucking tone. That 'you're overreacting and wasting my time, kid,' tone.

"Why aren't you taking this seriously?"

His scowl deepens, irritation flickering in his beady eyes.

Fuck him. My patience ran out over an hour ago.

Reaching beneath the counter, he pulls out a form and shoves it across the desk to me. "You know what, kid?" he snaps. "Here. Have at it."

My gaze drops to the paperwork, my eyes skimming over the text.

"Once twenty-four hours have passed, you can file a missing person's report." He glowers. "This will help you get a head start on the paperwork. You can turn it in once twenty-four hours have passed, not a minute before."

My nostrils flare, and my fingers curl around the papers.

Fuck this guy and his fucking form. This isn't going to help me find her.

"You and the girl both attend PacNorth, right?"

I nod, barely holding back my fury. I cannot lunge across this counter. I cannot punch this *pendejo* in the face. Cecilia needs me right now, and I cannot—under any circumstance—get myself arrested.

"She's probably with her girlfriends or at one of those fraternity parties you kids are always excited about. I'm sure your friend will turn up, and you won't even need the paperwork."

Grinding my teeth, I fight to rein in my temper. "What about the whole bit where every minute counts in a missing person's case? The first forty-eight hours are crucial, and if we wait—"

"That only applies if the individual is missing."

She is missing! I want to scream.

Fuck this. I'm getting nowhere.

"Thanks for nothing," I snap, grabbing the paper from the countertop and storming outside where the rest of the guys are waiting for me.

Felix pushes off the hood of his car, his face tense with worry as soon as I shove through the glass doors. "What'd they say?" he hollers.

Jaw tight, I stride toward him. "They won't look for her. It hasn't been long enough since we last saw her, and they don't think she's actually missing. The asshole had the nerve to suggest she's out partying right now."

"That's bullshit," Atticus exclaims, his hands clenched into fists at his sides. "Cecilia wouldn't be caught dead at a party."

"I know." I fold the missing person's form and slide it into my back pocket before accepting the helmet Julio holds out for me.

"So, if the cops won't help, what's the plan?" Julio asks, his expression grim.

"I don't know." I tighten my grip on the helmet. The weight of the last 24 hours crashes down on me. What was I thinking? Going off on her like that. I was mean to her.

Nah. My mouth twists thinking about the words I said. "Mean" is being too generous. What I really was is cruel. I told her shit between us is over when it isn't. I lashed out and knew how

4

hard each verbal blow would land. Cecilia didn't deserve that. And now she's MIA, all because of me.

I hang my head as a fresh wave of shame settles over me. I was just so fucking angry. Seeing the way my mom looked at me—the way she rejected my very existence in her life ... It hurt. But that's not an excuse. I let family shit get in my head, and I took it out on someone I care about. I fucked up. So what if Mom wants nothing to do with me? It's been like that for a while now. Ever since my twin's death. I should be used to it by now. I might not have predicted how shitty her rejection would feel, but I knew, deep down, she didn't want me there. That the invitation had to be some sort of fluke. A mistake. And then I went and made an already shitty night shittier by blaming Cecilia. By lashing out and pushing the one woman who actually gives a damn about me away.

I don't know what the hell I was thinking. Now Holt's made bail. What is it going to be next?

"We could try the pool again," Deacon suggests, his tone doubtful.

I pull my helmet down over my head and flick up the visor. "You do that," I tell him. "It can't hurt." But it's not like he'll find her there. We've already looked. Deacon is just trying to be useful. To stay busy. We all are. The more time that passes, the harder it is not to think of all the worst-case scenarios. But, I can't go there yet. My stomach is already sick with dread. I have to believe she's okay. That Holt didn't find some way to get to her.

"What if she really isn't missing?" Felix hedges, his voice uncertain. "She was upset. You guys had just had a fight. She might have gone somewhere to clear her head. It's what you did when you disappeared to the Pier. Maybe she—"

5

"When she needs to clear her head, she goes to the campus pool. She swims. She's got a pool at her place and we have the pool at PacNorth. She's not at either of them. We've looked everywhere else she frequents. J called Adriana. She doesn't know where Cecilia is. She called around to some of the other girls on the swim team, and they hadn't seen her either. Fuck, I even reached out to that asswipe, Wyatt, that she went out with before. I don't know where else she would go." My voice sounds defeated even to my own ears.

"We'll go sit on Holt's house," Atticus suggests, indicating Deacon beside him. "We'll swing by the campus pool on our way just to be safe. Someone should have eyes on Holt in case he leaves or ..." He trails off with a shrug.

"Yeah. Okay. Thanks." The two of them head out in Atticus's car, leaving Julio, Felix, and me alone in the police parking lot.

"You should take a beat," Julio says. "It's been a few hours. You need—"

"I need to find her," I grit out. "That's all that matters right now."

Julio purses his lips together. "She was upset when Felix dropped her off," he reminds me. "I get that swimming is her thing, but she still might have gone somewhere else. For a walk or to a friend's."

"She doesn't hang out with anyone else. She's got us, and she has Adriana. That's it."

I know Julio is trying to be reasonable. He probably thinks I'm overreacting, but I'm not. I can't explain it. But I know it in my gut. Cecilia isn't okay. It's the same feeling I had during our practice that something was wrong. I was right then. And I know I'm right now.

6

Julio sighs. "Fine. We'll figure out where to look next after we drop your bike off at the soccer house. We'll use the drive over to brainstorm ideas."

"We should split—"

"No," Julio cuts me off. "We did that already. We divided, and we didn't conquer. You're running on fumes, and I don't need you racing off on your bike in the middle of the night and getting yourself killed. Follow us home, drop off the bike. We'll regroup and then take Felix's car to continue the search."

"Fine." I throw a leg over my CBR 1000, settling onto the leather seat. Flipping over the ignition, the engine roars to life. I tug on my riding gloves and rev the engine, preparing to head out, when Felix steps up beside me.

"Keep your head on straight, and don't do anything stupid." He raises his voice to be heard over the motor. "We're all worried, okay? But we're gonna find her."

He claps me on the shoulder, and I grunt.

"I'll see you at the house in ten. Don't take any detours." Flicking my visor down, I brush off the order and take off down the street, the wind whipping around me as I race toward the soccer house. My heart pounds in my chest, determination fueling me. I want to believe him. There's no alternative.

I am going to find her. And she's going to be okay.

She has to be.

two

CECILIA

Five hours earlier

FELIX PULLS UP in front of my house, the silence in the car heavy as I look up at the illuminated front porch. It's early evening—not quite dark yet—but it will be in another hour or so. Our neighborhood is quiet, the kind of suburban tranquility that hides secrets behind closed doors. The streetlamps flicker on as the sky darkens, casting long shadows across the manicured lawns and perfectly trimmed hedges. It's almost too perfect, like a scene from a movie set.

My parents' cars sit in the driveway letting me know they're home.

Terrific.

"Do you want me to ...?" Felix's voice trails off, soft and uncertain. He's looking at me, then at the house like he knows what I'm thinking but doesn't know how to say it.

"No. It's fine," I say, swallowing down the tightness in my throat. "I'm good."

He nods, but his frown doesn't disappear. "If you change your mind ..."

I shake my head. "I won't, but thanks."

Felix doesn't owe me anything. He's Gabriel's friend, not mine. He already gave me a ride home, and that's more than enough. I can't ask him for more. I won't.

Unbuckling my seatbelt, I hesitate, staring down at the still-dark screen of my phone. No new messages. No calls. The longer the silence, the harder it gets to fight the growing knot in my stomach.

We're fine. He's mad, sure, but we're fine. "We *have* to be fine." I whisper the words under my breath, as if saying them aloud will make it true. I'm trying not to blow up Gabriel's phone, but every minute that passes without a word from him makes it that much harder.

The drive from the wedding to my place was only twenty minutes. More than enough time for him to realize I didn't mean for tonight to happen the way it did, right? He knows I wouldn't hurt him intentionally. Not ever. If I'd known the way his mom would react, I never would have pushed him to go.

"Call me if you need anything," Felix says, his voice breaking into my thoughts as I open the car door. "You have my number, right?"

I freeze. "Uh, yeah." I don't, but I lie because why would I have Felix's number?

Felix doesn't move, though, just stares at me with that same look until I sigh and hand him my phone. He taps away at the screen for a few seconds, then hands it back.

"I saved all our numbers. Mine, Julio's, Deacon's, Atticus's. The whole crew. Call if you need anything."

"I could sell that, you know?" I say in a failed attempt to lighten the mood. "I could probably pay this semester's tuition with the number of girls who want that kind of access to you guys."

He snorts, but his eyes soften. "You won't."

"You sure about that?" I jest.

The corners of his eyes crinkle. "Yeah, Cecilia. I am." He gives me a knowing look. "You're one of us," he says. "And family doesn't turn on their own."

My chest tightens in a way I didn't expect. "Well, thanks," I mutter, not knowing what else to say.

Stepping out, I close the door behind me, but before I've taken more than one step, Felix rolls down the passenger side window.

"He's crazy about you," Felix adds, softer this time. "Just ... sometimes the timing isn't right, you know?"

My throat feels thick, and I blink back the sudden moisture in my eyes. "Yeah. I know."

"Get some rest," Felix says, his voice calm, yet firm, as though he's issuing an order. "Timing for you two might be shit, but all that means is you guys have more ups and downs than most. Give him some space. He'll come around when he's ready."

I want to believe him, but doubt gnaws its way into the pit of my stomach. "Thanks," I manage.

I know Felix is just being nice, but I wish he wouldn't. I wish he'd just be honest with me.

When he first showed up tonight, he said what Gabe and I are doing, that it isn't healthy. This back and forth rollercoaster ride we're on—together one minute and pushing each other away the next—it's not good for either one of us. And I hate that it's true and that he isn't the first to say that to me. Julio said almost the exact same thing a handful of weeks ago.

So why tell me that he'll come around? Why get my hopes up if neither of them think we should even be together?

But what am I supposed to do? Allow Gabriel to push me away when he's hurting? Prove him right by leaving when things get tough? How does that help anyone?

For what feels like the hundredth time, I think about calling Gabe. I want to. I *need* to. But he's made it clear he doesn't want to talk. Not now. If I push him before he's ready, I'll only make things worse. I keep hearing his parting words over and over in my head. *It's over. I'm done. I don't want to be your fucking friend.*

How do we recover from that?

"You've got my number now," Felix says, interrupting my spiraling thoughts. "Use it if you need it."

"Yeah. Okay. Thanks."

I wave him off, but he doesn't leave right away. "You going inside?" he asks, raising an eyebrow.

"In a couple minutes." I sigh. "Just ... need to get my head on straight first, you know?"

12

Felix's lips press together before he nods. "My mom would kill me if she knew I left you out here alone."

"I'm fine. Really. I just need a few minutes. Promise."

He hesitates, then relents. "Only a few minutes. You swear?"

I raise two fingers. "Scout's honor. I'm a big girl."

With a roll of his eyes, Felix shifts into drive. "Take care, Cecilia."

I watch him go, standing there until his taillights disappear around the corner. Then it's just me, the shadows, and the hollow ache in my chest. *It's going to be okay.* I repeat it over and over, trying to convince myself it's the truth.

Giving Gabriel space is the right thing to do. An easy thing, really. One that requires zero effort on my part.

So why does it feel impossible?

Gabriel told me to back off, and I'm going to respect that.

My fingers tighten around my phone. I hate this. Hate that I'm spiraling, obsessing, waiting for a call that's not going to come tonight. It shouldn't hurt this much. It shouldn't feel like we're at opposite ends of the world growing further and further away from one another.

But it does.

Why is this so freaking hard?

It's not like we were *together* together. We weren't dating. I'm getting so worked up when this doesn't have to be a thing.

We tried the friends-with-benefits thing. It didn't work. Then we tried just being friends.

13

Clearly that also failed.

Maybe the best thing for the both of us really is a clean break.

But the thought of losing Gabriel ... I can't. I'm not ready for that. Maybe that's selfish, but I don't care. I don't know how to quit him. And even if I did, I don't think I could go through with it.

I take a few steps toward the front door, but anxiety sinks its claws into my chest.

My parents. Shit.

Mom knows I went with Gabriel to the wedding. She was practically giddy when I left. She doesn't know where we stand now, but she's aware things have been rocky between us, especially after the whole Austin ordeal. She asks about him a lot—always eager to remind me how he hasn't been around as much. Gabriel is the dream package to her, and I get it, he's amazing. But it's complicated, way more complicated than she thinks.

Tonight, she was so excited that I was "giving him another chance." Her words, not mine. If I walk in right now, she'll know something's off. It's only been an hour since I left. The questions will start before I even close the door.

Why are you home so early?

Where's Gabriel?

Why didn't he walk you to the door?

Is everything okay?

Did you two have a fight?

Why do you look like you've been crying?

14

I'd have to tell her what happened because I'm too tired and emotionally drained to come up with a plausible lie. And if I tell her the truth, she'll freak out. Dad will be dragged into it, and suddenly, my mental health will become their main concern. Mom'll suggest calling my therapist—just to be safe—and then it'll become a whole thing.

No. I can't deal with that. Not tonight. Not after everything else.

I take a step back, my chest tightening, the air feeling too thick. Shit. Not now, Cecilia. Get it together.

But the panic keeps building, clawing at my insides. My heart races, my breaths come too fast, too shallow. I can see my dad's worried face already, the fear in my mom's eyes.

Clenching my fists, I try to focus. Breathe. In through the nose, out through the mouth. Hold it. One ... two ... three ... four seconds.

I do it again. Then again.

It's not working.

My nails dig into the fabric of my dress, the soft satin-like material crumpling between my fingers as I grip tighter. It's damp from the sweat on my palms. I squeeze my eyes shut, willing the tension in my chest to release. The pressure feels like a weight pressing down, making it hard to breathe.

Okay, new plan. Senses.

My therapist said to focus on my senses. One by one.

I open my eyes and latch onto the porch. Visuals first. Rocking chair. There's a faint creak it makes as the wind pushes it back and forth. Red flowers in a ceramic pot, bright against the grey backdrop of the day. The brick steps—solid, worn, reliable beneath my feet. The wood door. Sturdy. A barrier between me and the chaos inside my head.

I shift, feeling the coolness of the breeze brush over my skin, goosebumps rising in its wake. Touch. The way the fabric of my dress sticks to my thighs, wrinkling under my hands as I smooth it down, trying to focus on the texture. It's soft, familiar. I rub my thumb over it again, needing the anchor.

Sound. There's a faint rustle of leaves, the distant hum of traffic, the chirp of a bird somewhere off in the distance. The world outside moves at its own pace, indifferent to the storm swirling inside me.

Slowly, the pressure in my chest begins to ease. My heartbeat, which had been hammering wildly, starts to slow, each thud a hair less frantic than the last.

The dizziness fades.

I'm okay.

I've got this.

I glance down at my phone again. Still nothing. The knot in my stomach tightens, but I shove the phone back in my pocket. Maybe I'll take a walk to clear my head before going inside. Just as I start to turn around, the door swings open.

Dad steps out, dressed in his business suit, his tie loose, phone pressed to his ear. He glances at me, surprised, but holds up a finger, mouthing, "One sec."

I nod, forcing a small smile while he wraps up his call. Something about a meeting that ran late.

When he hangs up, he looks me over quickly, but doesn't ask any of the questions I'd been dreading. "Hey, kiddo. Didn't expect you home so soon. How was the wedding?"

I manage to shrug casually. "It was … good. I actually just forgot something so I'm uh … gonna run in and grab that."

He nods, clearly distracted as he tucks his phone into his pocket. "Alright, kiddo. Your mom had a charity dinner tonight, and I'm running late to pick her up. We should be back in about an hour. You want us to bring you anything for dinner?"

I shake my head, feeling a wave of relief wash over me. I don't have to explain anything. Not yet. "No, I'm good. Just grabbing a few things," I say, hoping that's enough to satisfy him.

"Alright," he says, already halfway down the driveway. "See you soon."

I watch him climb into his car and pull away, my heart still hammering, but with a bit of space to breathe now. Thank god for small miracles. At least I don't have to face the inevitable onslaught of questions yet.

But I can't stay here, waiting for Mom to come back. She'll notice everything Dad missed. My red eyes. The tightness in my voice. She'll dig deeper than Dad did, and I don't have the energy to deflect her.

I need to get out of here. Right. The walk. Fresh air. Maybe then, I'll be able to think straight.

At the very least, it will kill some time. Long enough so that when I go inside, I can smile and pretend the wedding was terrific. That Gabriel and I had a great time. With a quick glance down the darkening street, I start walking.

three
CECILIA

THE QUIET STREET feels like it's closing in. I keep walking, arms wrapped tightly around myself. The night breeze cuts through my dress like it's nothing, the chill settling deep into my bones. I catch a flicker of movement out of the corner of my eye—a stray cat maybe, or just a trick of the light—but the unease inside me only digs deeper. It's getting dark and it's getting dark fast.

Twenty minutes into my walk, I know I made a mistake. My feet drag across the pavement, the stillness amplifying everything: my own thoughts, the echo of Gabriel's face when his mom had asked him, flat out, what he was doing there. The look of utter defeat that followed.

It broke something inside him, and I watched it happen like a front-row spectator. His mom, wrapped up in her new family, didn't even seem to care that he existed anymore. How do you deal with that? I can't imagine what it would feel like to be rejected by a parent so completely. To be *replaced*. And Gabriel? God, he's amazing. He's kind and thoughtful. He always puts the people he cares about first, and he's loyal to a fault. Hell, even pissed off at me, he still made sure to call Felix to give me a ride home. And he waited. He didn't want to talk to me, but he stuck around long enough for Felix to show up so I wasn't left alone. Who doesn't want someone like that in their life?

"A crazy person," I mutter under my breath.

The street is eerily silent, and my footsteps sound too loud against the pavement. The rustling leaves only add to the tension building under my skin. I wrap my arms tighter, trying to ward off the chill creeping down my spine, when my ears pick up the low rumble of an approaching engine.

I glance over my shoulder, catching sight of a blacked-out Audi Q8 creeping up behind me, its windows too dark to see through. My brows knit together. I don't recognize it, and a vehicle like that stands out in a neighborhood like this. We're nice, but not *Audi Q8* nice.

I shrug it off, but a minute later, the SUV is still there, hovering a few car lengths back, moving with me. My stomach clenches. I step up onto the edge of someone's lawn—no sidewalks on this part of the street—and slow my steps, waiting for it to pass.

It doesn't.

What the hell?

My heart skips a beat, a chill creeping up the back of my neck. The car is still following, still keeping pace with me. Maybe they're looking for a house number? That's all it is. No reason to freak out.

I glance over my shoulder again. No, something's off. The car slows, deliberately matching my pace. My chest tightens, my breaths coming a little quicker now. *Shit. Don't freak out. Austin's in jail. You have a restraining order against Parken and Gregroy. You're fine.*

I try to speed up, my feet slapping against the pavement faster now, sandals scraping the ground. My pulse quickens with every second the car doesn't pass. *Better safe than sorry,* I think, *any second now they'll pull into a driveway, and I'll feel stupid for even thinking this.*

But they don't. My hands tremble, heart pounding in my ears. The car is still there.

Shit. Shit. Shit.

I fumble for my phone, the device slipping through my sweaty fingers. I let out a frustrated, "Fuck!" as it hits the pavement with a crack. Bending down to grab it, the Audi suddenly surges ahead, swerving in front of me, cutting me off.

Panic seizes my chest. My pulse pounds like a drumbeat in my head as I clutch my phone, eyes glued to the car. I take a step back. Then another.

I'm not that far from home. Two blocks. Maybe three. I could make it. My shoes aren't meant for running, but who cares? I could make it if I have to. *No one's going to grab you, Cecilia. Don't be ridiculous.*

But fear wraps around me, suffocating.

The rear door swings open, and I freeze, every muscle in my body going rigid. A woman steps out, her bright red heels hitting the pavement first, followed by long, elegant legs. She's tall, blonde, and immaculately dressed in a red pencil skirt and matching blazer. Not exactly the image of a kidnapper.

Relief trickles in, but it doesn't last long. There's something off in the way she looks at me—intense, sharp, like she's calculating something. I shift on my feet, suddenly unsure.

"Cecilia Russo?" Her voice is like ice, slicing through the night air.

I blink, trying to make sense of what's happening. I don't respond at first, too busy scanning her face, her posture. She's older, closer to my mom's age. Something about her feels familiar, but I can't place it.

She arches a brow, clearly annoyed by my silence. "That *is* your name, isn't it?"

"Uh, yeah. That's me," I stammer, my throat dry as I meet her gaze. Where do I know her from?

The woman gives a curt nod, lips pulling into a tight smile. "Jaymin Holt," she says. *Holt*. The name hits like a punch to the gut.

Austin's mother.

I take a step back, instinctively. "What do you want?" My voice shakes.

"To talk about Austin," she says smoothly, like that explains everything. As if hearing his name doesn't make my skin crawl.

Panic pulses under my skin. I should have run. But now I'm stuck, frozen in place as she takes a step closer.

"I won't take much of your time," she continues, gesturing to the open door of the SUV. "Please."

There's something in her tone, like saying 'please' costs her something. My instincts scream at me to get away, but I force myself to stay still. *If I remember correctly, she's a lawyer. She isn't going to assault me or do anything illegal, right?* Right.

I just need to look at this logically. She wants to talk, but I don't have to listen to her. I can say no and walk away. Everyone here is reasonable.

Then the driver's door opens, and my heart races all over again. A man steps out—tall, broad-shouldered, with the kind of presence that demands attention. His eyes are cold, assessing, as they land on me. He moves with the kind of careful, precise motions I've only seen from fighters or military types.

He nods once at Jaymin and strides around the SUV, coming to stand beside her.

"Get in the car, Ms. Russo," he says, voice low and authoritative. It's not a suggestion.

I swallow hard. "I think I'm good here, thanks."

His expression doesn't change. "That would be a mistake."

I take a small step back, pulse racing. My brain screams at me to run, but every instinct tells me I won't get far. Not with the way he's watching me, poised to react.

"Mrs. Holt is being patient," the driver says. "But *my* patience is running thin. I suggest you accept her invitation."

I glance at Jaymin, whose smile has all but vanished. "I just want to talk," she says, her tone brittle. "Ten minutes. Then you can be on your way."

I weigh my options, chewing on my lip.

"You won't like what happens if you try to run," the driver says.

"Are you threatening me?" I ask. My eyes flick from him to Jaymin.

"She's not," the driver says. "But if that's what you need in order to comply, then sure." He shrugs. "I guess I am."

Alright then. Glad we cleared that up.

Guess I don't really have a lot of options here. I take a shaky breath and force myself to step forward. "Ten minutes," I say, my voice barely above a whisper.

I slide into the backseat, the cool leather chilling my skin. Jaymin follows, settling in beside me, her eyes sharp and unwavering. The driver gets in, and with a quiet *click*, the doors lock.

My heart stutters as I grip my phone tight, praying this conversation is just that—a conversation.

"I shouldn't be here," I tell her. "My attorney wouldn't want me talking to you."

The SUV pulls away from the curb, and I try not to think about all those lovely little murder statistics about women who are taken to second locations. I should really cut back on the number of true crime episodes I watch.

"We're just going to have a friendly little chat," Jaymin tells me. "I'm sure he won't mind."

I disagree but keep my thoughts to myself. Despite saying she wants to talk, Jaymin sits quietly beside me.

My skin itches the longer we go without speaking, but I refuse to be the one to break the silence. She's the one who wanted this little meet and greet. Not me.

Shifting in her seat, Jaymin crosses one elegant leg over the other before finally turning to face me. "I'd like for the two of us to get our stories straight. I think you'll find it beneficial if we're both on the same page."

Déjà vu washes over me, and it's like I'm there. Back in that room. Scared and confused as I take in my torn clothes and the bruises on my skin. Then Austin opens the door and says almost the exact same thing. *Let's get our stories straight.*

No single sentence has ever triggered me more.

four

CECILIA

PANIC LODGES IN MY THROAT, thick and unyielding. I am not doing this. I can't. What was I thinking getting into this car? I should have run. God, I'm an idiot. Why didn't I run?

To hell if her driver chases me. At least if I ran, I'd have a chance. I remember reading that the odds of surviving an abduction plummet once a victim is taken to a second location. Something like seventy-five percent of abductions end in murder if the victim is moved.

Shit. Shit. Shit.

Why am I only just now remembering that statistic from that stupid true crime podcast Adriana made me listen to with her? I've just royally screwed myself over.

My stomach churns with a sudden, sickening realization. Oh god. What if this is their plan to get rid of me? What if "we need to talk" is code for "we need to make it easier to dispose of the body?"

Jaymin's plan to get Austin off could be to get rid of me. It's as simple as that. No victim, no charges. Right?

My fingers fumble for the handle, trembling so hard I can barely grasp it. But just like I thought they would be, the child locks are already engaged.

"Let me out." My voice is strained, a desperate whisper as panic settles over me like a second skin, suffocating and tight. The SUV's interior is a black cage, the air thick with tension and the oppressive scent of luxury. Jaymin's sharp blue eyes bore into mine, amplifying my fear. God. Her eyes are just like his.

I rattle the handle again, my breaths coming in short, stuttered gasps. "I'm serious," I say to no one in particular. "Let me out of the car."

My eyes dart to the gap between the front seats. There's a small sliver of hope. Child locks only work on the rear doors, right? I could slip between the seats and—

"Ms. Russo—"

I don't answer her. My mind conjures possible routes of escape before quickly discarding them one after the other. Think, Cecilia. Think.

"Ms. Russo—" She reaches a hand toward me.

"Don't touch me!" I snap, my voice on the edge of hysteria.

My hands are shaking uncontrollably now. A high-pitched ringing fills my ears, threatening to drown out everything else. My field of vision narrows as the weight of the situation crashes over me. I can't breathe. With my phone still in my hand, I clutch at my chest.

Not again. I will not be somebody else's unwilling victim again.

I glance at the driver—his eyes cold and impassive in the rearview mirror—then back to Jaymin. The driver is the more obvious threat, but Jaymin is the one in charge. Her authority is almost tangible in the confined space, pressing in around me on all sides. I'm suffocating, the walls of the SUV closing in.

"Let me out!" I scream. "Screw getting our stories straight. I don't need to be on whatever page of crazy you happen to be on." So much for being reasonable.

My vision blurs. Don't pass out. Do. Not. Pass. Out. "Fuck. You're just like him, aren't you?" I'm hyperventilating. "Austin's the way he is because of you."

My words hang in the air between us, and Jaymin's nostrils flare. The only indication that my words had any effect on her.

"Are you done?" she asks, her words clipped.

My chest rises and falls at a rapid rate because no, I'm not done. But shit, what are my options here?

The SUV's engine hums around me, a mechanical beast ready to swallow me whole. I ignore Jaymin's question and retrieve my phone from the floor mat where I must have dropped it. I press my finger on the power button. "Come on. Come on." The screen illuminates. Yes!

I wait for the home screen to load, my knee bouncing with impatience when Jaymin plucks the device from my fingertips. I lunge for it but not before the driver shoves an arm between the seats, effectively knocking me back.

"Give that back!"

Jaymin ignores me. Tucking my phone into the purse beside her feet, she glares down her nose at me. I consider diving for it. But then what?

"My patience is wearing thin, Ms. Russo. I recommend you pull yourself together so we can get this conversation over with."

I force myself to breathe, each inhalation shallow and quick.

Jaymin's eyes are narrowed. "You're making this harder than it needs to be, Cecilia. Austin is out on bail. Get yourself together so we can discuss what needs to happen next."

Her words hit me like a punch to the gut, knocking the air out of my lungs. "What?" Disbelief and horror mingle into one sickening cocktail. "He made bail?" How the hell did he make bail?

The officer who took my statement said he wouldn't. That given the severity of his crime and the clear motive and evidence, he wouldn't be afforded the opportunity before trial.

Was the officer mistaken? Or did he lie?

Jaymin's gaze is steady, her lips pressing into a thin line. "Yes. He made bail," she repeats, each word a dagger of cold reality. "I need you to listen to me very carefully."

I swallow hard, my pulse racing. But the shock of her revelation has cut through my panic like a knife.

"Austin was released this afternoon. But, he didn't come home. My husband is in the process of locating him now, which is why—"

"You think he'll come after me again?"

Her jaw tightens. "My son is angry. But he isn't an idiot." Not sure I agree with that statement. Austin did try to drown me on campus with cameras and witnesses after all. "His anger may have clouded his judgment before, but I do not believe him so unreasonable as to allow his anger to override him again. No. This—" she indicates the space between us, "—is merely a precaution until my husband is able to determine our son's whereabouts."

She's kidding herself if she believes that. "How long are you going to force me to stay here?"

She sighs and looks away. "As long as is necessary. I suggest you get comfortable." So much for ten minutes.

five

CECILIA

"PULL AROUND BACK," Jaymin says to her driver, her voice low but with the kind of authority that doesn't invite discussion. As the SUV shifts into reverse, moving down a narrow alley, I catch a flicker of dread in the pit of my stomach. The alley dead-ends, brick walls rising on either side like a tomb closing in around me. I peer out the tinted window, trying to pinpoint where we are, but nothing here looks familiar. Richland isn't that big of a town, but this... this is unfamiliar territory.

The engine cuts off, leaving an eerie silence, and I feel the weight of it press against my chest. Jaymin unbuckles her seatbelt with a slow, deliberate click, her manicured nails tapping against the console before resting in her lap. The locks are still engaged. My breath catches. I listen for that telltale *click* of the doors unlocking, but it doesn't come. Instead, the driver's eyes meet mine in the rearview mirror—dark, impassive, waiting.

Swallowing hard, I try the door handle, pushing with my shoulder.

It doesn't budge.

Shit.

I shove against it again. This time a little harder.

Nothing.

Jaymin sighs softly, as though mildly inconvenienced by my panic. The driver, without a word, opens his door. The dull thud echoes in the narrow alley, and my pulse kicks up a notch. When he rounds the car and yanks my door open, I almost stumble out. His large frame blocks the exit, towering over me with a blank expression, as though this is just another Tuesday afternoon for him. Keys jingle in his hand, a subtle reminder of who's in control here.

"If you'll follow me," he says, his voice calm, too calm. His hand gestures toward the stone steps that lead to an old wooden door. But my legs refuse to move. I glance down the alley, weighing my chances. The walls feel like they're closing in. *How the hell do I get out of here?*

My mind runs a mile a minute while my body stands frozen on the pavement. His hand flexes, and he presses a button on the key fob. The locks disengage. Jaymin opens her door and steps out before I'm able to react.

"Miss?" With a huff, I step toward the driver and allow him to herd me toward the stone steps where Jaymin now stands. Her purse is clutched between her hands. The same purse that has my freaking cell phone in it. She climbs the steps before unlocking the heavy wood door and stepping inside. It's obvious Jaymin expects us to follow, but I don't. My sandaled feet are frozen on the bottom step as I stare up into the open doorway. Dread sits heavy in my stomach, the doorway like an open maw waiting to consume my soul as soon as I pass the threshold. Going inside is a mistake. And I've made enough mistakes for one day.

Taking a step back, I'm met by a large palm in the center of my back. Swallowing hard, I look up and over my shoulder at the driver. He has over a foot of height on me, and with him this close ... I suck in a ragged breath and step forward, putting some much-needed distance between us.

"You could just let me go," I mutter, my voice shaky but defiant. "Say I ran off, kicked you in the balls, whatever. It could work." Please. I silently pray. Just say yes. Say you'll let me go.

The corner of his mouth twitches like he's fighting back a smile, but there's no humor in his eyes. He steps closer, his hand resting firmly on the small of my back, and my breath catches in my throat. I can feel the warmth of his body, the press of authority in that simple touch. I'm being herded like cattle up the steps and through the open door.

As we ascend the steps, dread builds, pooling low in my belly. The wooden door creaks open, revealing Jaymin who is seated in the formal sitting area.

Her red-manicured nails drum against the arm of the sofa. There's cold calculation in her gaze. "Have a seat," she says as soon as I step into the room.

"I'd rather stand," I tell her. "What is this place?" I'm halfway through the door when I feel the weight of the driver's hand leave my back. Too late to turn back now. My feet drag on the polished wood floors as I'm led deeper into what looks like a colonial-style sitting room, but everything here feels wrong.

The air is too still, the walls too clean. It smells faintly of pine and disinfectant, like someone wiped away any trace of life here. There are no photographs, no personal touches.

The sitting room is laid out more like a coworking space with three large wooden desks positioned against the back wall, each desktop neat and orderly. There are two more desks arranged on the opposite side of the room and a small bar top in one corner that's set up as a coffee station. In the center of the room is the sofa Jaymin sits on with a pair of masculine club chairs seated directly across from it and an ornate wooden coffee table nestled between them.

The walls themselves are painted a deep green with picture frame molding adorning each wall. It's pretty, something you might find in a magazine, but there's no warmth here. Just clean lines and a cold, professional sterility.

"This is one of my company's properties. Mostly used by our associates. But, for today's purposes, it will serve as a waiting room." Her voice is smooth, but there's a sharpness underneath, like a blade hidden in silk. "Please, make yourself comfortable."

Comfortable? Right.

"I'm good," I bite out, my arms folding across my chest as I take a step closer to the window. The glass feels cold beneath my fingertips, the world outside so close and yet so far away.

"Very well." Jaymin's eyes narrow slightly, but her expression doesn't change. She leans back into the plush cushions, unbothered. "While we wait, I believe it's prudent to discuss the pending charges against my son and what you can expect should this move to trial."

She's kidding, right?

I laugh, but there's no humor in it. "You're my rapist's mother." The words spill out before I can stop them, venom coating every syllable. "Pretty sure it wouldn't be *prudent* to talk to you about anything."

Her lips press together in a thin line, but she doesn't flinch. "There are no charges of rape being brought against Austin," she reminds me coolly, her tone clipped.

"Right. My bad." My voice cracks with sarcasm. "It's attempted murder this time around. I sometimes get all of the times your son has attacked me a little muddled. You know, since there are so many."

She huffs out a breath as I fight to keep hold of my temper. The anger at least helps keep the panic at bay.

"I understand you have a tumultuous relationship with my son," she says, her voice as cold as the room around us.

I snort. Tumultuous? The word grates on my nerves like nails on a chalkboard. "Austin hurt me," I say flatly, my voice cutting through the air like glass. "He held me down while his friends drugged and assaulted me. He laughed while they did it and then he raped me himself," I grind the words out through gritted teeth. Then, when I told the University what happened, you and your husband stepped in and defended him. You threw your weight and money around and made it all go away. He didn't even get a slap on the wrist. No suspension. Nothing."

Jaymin's expression remains blank, unbothered. Her gaze stays steady, cool and collected, like none of this is affecting her in the slightest.

My eyes screw shut as angry tears burn the backs of my eyelids.

"I'm—"

"No," I grit my teeth, the anger bubbling up again, white-hot and suffocating. I need her to understand everything her son has done to me and that she's played a role in it. "You didn't just protect him—you enabled him. You made him invulnerable. Whatever worries or doubts Austin might have had, whatever consequences he may have braced himself for, it all went away. You showed him he could hurt people and get away with it. That being called out for his crimes was nothing more than a minor inconvenience that money could easily sweep away. So, of course, he didn't stop there."

Tearing my gaze from the window, I turn to face her, my anger and frustration mounting. Does she see her own complicity in all of this? "After he got away with it, he taunted me. He took every opportunity to throw his actions in my face and told anyone who would listen how much of a slut I am. He said I retaliated with lies after being stung by his rejection. He made people hate me. My own friends turned their backs on me." I pause just long enough to catch my breath. "Austin took everything from me. Every shred of my dignity. And it still wasn't enough."

The silence in the room is deafening. My heart is pounding in my chest, my pulse so loud in my ears that I can barely hear myself think. I want to scream, to throw something, but I know it won't make a difference. Jaymin won't crack.

"Your son took pleasure in my discomfort. In my pain. When I didn't give him the reaction he wanted, he picked and poked and prodded some more. He threatened to silence me for good and slammed my head into a brick wall on campus when he thought I told one of his teammates what he did to me. Spoiler alert, I didn't," I bite out. "And then he tried to drown me in a fucking swimming pool after his own actions got him kicked off the team."

Adrenaline floods my veins just thinking about that day. I didn't think I was going to make it. He held me down for so long ...

I watch her face closely, waiting—hoping—for some sign of guilt, some flicker of regret in her cold eyes, but there's nothing. Her expression is like stone.

"Tumultuous is putting it mildly, but no, I have no relationship with your son. He is my attacker, and I, his unwilling victim. Nothing more."

"I sympathize with what you've been through."

I snort. Sure, she does.

Jaymin's lips press into a thin line, her gaze dropping for a split second before returning to mine. "I didn't come here to fight with you," she says, her voice calm but firm. "I came here to prepare you. You deserve to know what's going to happen next."

I blink, the confusion cutting through my rage like ice water. "Prepare me? For what?"

six

CECILIA

"MY SON WON'T BE TRIED for rape," she tells me.

My jaw tightens. "I'm aware," I tell her. He and the others already got away with what they did to me. Assuming anyone bothered to believe me now, there's no evidence. I never got a rape kit. I didn't save the clothes. It's been almost a year now since the assault, and at this point, it's just my word against his. I already know how that goes.

"But he did try to kill me, and he was stupid enough to do it on campus where the surveillance cameras caught him."

She sighs and settles back into her seat. "Yes. I'm aware."

"He's going to prison." There's no way Austin can talk his way out of it. Not this time.

A muscle in her jaw ticks. "That's what I wanted to discuss with you."

"No."

"Excuse me?"

"You're going to ask me to drop the charges. That's my answer. No. Austin has spent the better part of a year doing everything he can to ruin my life. That man will get zero sympathy from me. I hope they throw the fucking book at him. He deserves to rot in a cell for what he did."

When I finish, my chest is heaving. Anger simmers beneath the surface of my skin. Jaymin is quiet for several seconds, and it's obvious she's mulling over her response.

"Have you gone to trial before, Ms. Russo? Have you witnessed court proceedings beyond what you've seen on television?"

Shaking my head, I keep my eyes cast out the window.

"Allow me to walk you through what comes next." There's a haughtiness to her voice, one that says she's about to teach me a lesson. "Austin may have been arrested, but there will still be an investigation. This can take anywhere from three to four months. After which, the charges will be reevaluated and either confirmed or modified. There will be an initial hearing and plea followed by any pre-trial motions and discovery. This can take another six to nine months."

The blood drains from my face. Nine months? On top of another three to four?

"Then we will conduct jury selection. This will be another month. The trial itself will take two to three months where you will be expected to testify."

Nausea rolls in the pit of my stomach.

"It will not be pleasant. For the victims, it never is.

Once the trial is complete, you'll wait through jury deliberation until a verdict can be met. The decision must be unanimous, and Ms. Russo, I don't believe you'll receive the verdict you're after."

My breath hitches.

"My son is a very charismatic boy with a bright future ahead of him. Juries don't like convicting people like him, but," she shrugs as if to say she doesn't have a care in the world, "it can happen. This adds another week after which if he is found guilty, he will be sentenced approximately one month later. All of that is to say that you will not see my son behind bars for at least a year, though it can take up to two. And I assure you as both his mother and legal counsel, I will do everything in my power to prevent and delay that fate. If convicted, there will be appeals. You will go through the trial process all over again if necessary."

No. I—

Grinding my teeth together, I manage to force out my question. "What's the point in telling me all of this?" I knew this wouldn't be easy. Nothing with Austin is ever easy. But ... I didn't expect all of this. *A year? Maybe two?*

Hasn't Austin taken enough of my life as it is?

"The point is to ensure you have a full understanding of what you are entering into. Despite the evidence, this case will not be swift. It will be time-consuming and exhaustive. You will be forced to relive your trauma for public consumption. There will be media. Your father is a prominent member of the community, and my family is well known and well respected. Every news outlet will want an exclusive and we will give it to them because in the court of public opinion, perception matters. You will be hounded relentlessly. Every mistake you've made, every skeleton in your, or your family's, closet, they will all be brought to light.

The trial will put a strain on both your relationships and your studies, and in the end, it still may not result in a conviction."

Nausea churns in my gut. I knew all this, but hearing it said out loud ... "Wonderful. Thank you for this enlightening conversation."

"I'd like to save you that experience, Ms. Russo," Jaymin says. "If you'll let me."

I bark out a laugh. "Oh, really? And how is it that you'll manage that? Because you don't strike me as the type to just walk away and let your son rot for his crimes."

She purses her lips. "I'd like for us to discuss a plea deal. One that is mutually beneficial."

My eyes widen in disbelief. "You want to negotiate his freedom?"

There's a flicker of something in her eyes, but it's gone before I can really register what it is. Anger? Concern? I don't know.

"There are no winners in a case like this," she tells me. "Only compromises. If we can come to an agreement, we can both save ourselves months, if not years, of emotional turmoil and stress. I mean this to be a collaboration, Ms. Russo. We can both walk away from today's conversation with some level of satisfaction."

I highly doubt that.

"What are you proposing?" I already know whatever it is, I won't like it.

44

"Three years probation and a settlement in the amount of two-hundred and fifty thousand dollars to cover any pain and suffering you've endured."

My mouth drops open. Is she for real?

"You want to bribe me?"

Jaymin tuts. "Don't think of it as a bribe." She taps one finger against her chin. "Think of it as restitution for everything you've been through. A sum in this amount has the potential to significantly alter the course of your life. It could cover tuition. You can purchase your first home—"

"I don't care about any of that," I snap, cutting her off. "There is no amount of money in the world you can offer me that would make up for what he did. I'm not letting him buy his way out of this."

She purses her lips. "What is it that you want, then?"

"Jail time. That's my bare minimum." I won't settle for anything less.

"He is my son—"

"Then hold him accountable!"

Jaymin's eyes narrow and she considers me. "If we go to trial, there's a reasonable chance he could walk."

"I'm willing to take that chance," I tell her. "I won't settle for anything less than Austin behind bars."

"One year."

I choke on a laugh.

"Not good enough."

"Two, and we still provide you restitution. The same amount."

My heart races. Two years? No way. "No. Two years is nothing."

"Alright." She holds her arms out wide. "What do you want, then?"

Biting my lip I tell her, "Fifteen years."

Jaymin scoffs. "That's the maximum sentence for a second-degree murder charge. This is his first offense, and there is no evidence to show it was premeditated."

Bullshit.

"You asked me what I want. This is what I want. I want fifteen years."

She lets out a soft, almost mocking laugh. "Be realistic, Ms. Russo. We're both sensible adults here. Two years is more than fair."

"No."

"No?"

"You heard me. No."

"Are you aware of the sway the Holt name has in this town? Your father is already struggling simply by our withdrawal of financial support for his campaign." I bite my cheek until blood coats the back of my tongue. "Imagine the strain it would put on your parents if my husband and I decided to truly set our sights on them. I could bury both you and your family. I can make it unbearable for any of you to remain in Richland. All it would take are a few phone calls to the right people, and the entire lot of you would be run right out of town."

Ice slithers down my spine.

There she is. I knew the apple couldn't have fallen far from the tree.

"You could." I'm not naive. I know how much power Austin's family has. They helped him get away with raping me, after all. "But your son would still be in jail," I tell her. "You might bring me and my family down, but you'd lose too, and Austin behind bars would be satisfaction enough."

Jaymin bares her teeth. "Four years."

"No."

"You insolent little—" She takes a deep breath and gathers herself. "He is my son." There's a plea in her voice, but I'm not buying it.

"He is a monster."

"That may be," she confesses. "But he is mine. My monster. For better or worse, I will protect him."

Then she can go to hell with him.

"You're likely not aware of this, but Austin is adopted."

I wasn't aware, but I also don't see the point in telling me. He looks so much like his mother; it's hard to believe she didn't give birth to him. She must see the disbelief on my face.

"He's my nephew by blood," she tells me. "I had an older sister. We were never close. She went one direction in life, and I went the other." She looks away and picks at a thread in her skirt. "She died shortly after giving birth to Austin. Drug overdose," she confesses. "We'd already been estranged for years by that point, so I didn't know Austin existed until he was already four and had been bounced around the foster care system." She pauses to take a breath. "Nurture vs. nature. That's what all the experts say, right?" She laughs, but it isn't real. "I have loved that boy from the moment I laid my eyes on him. But, he had a hard start in life. And nurture can only overcome so much."

"Why are you telling me all of this?"

Does she expect me to empathize with him? Because I can't. I won't. Austin Holt is a monster. His mom dying and being in the system sucks, but there are plenty of people in the world born into shitty situations every day, and they don't grow up to become rapist assholes.

"I'm telling you so you understand where I'm coming from," she tells me. "I failed Austin those first few years. I wasn't there for him when he needed me. My son is not perfect, but I'm all he has in this world, and I won't allow him to become a product of his upbringing. What he did to you was wrong, but I won't abandon him when he needs me most. And I won't stand by while he rots away in a prison cell."

Our eyes lock, and it's on the tip of my tongue to tell her I don't care when she leans forward in her seat, her icy blue eyes holding mine.

"Five years, with the opportunity for parole. He'll serve jail time. That's what you said you wanted."

I shake my head. Five years isn't nearly enough, but ... she was right. Juries don't like to convict people like him. Austin Holt is the golden boy. Good-looking. Athletic. A model citizen in every sense if you ignore what he did to me. I'm his one black mark. That we know of at least. But with parole, there's a good chance he'd serve less time. Austin knows how to work the system.

"It isn't enough."

Her lips press into a thin line. "What if I can guarantee jail time for the other two boys who were involved?"

My spine straightens.

"How?" Gregory Chambers and Parker Benson were there that night. They ... did things to me. They participated. And later, when Austin tried to drown me, they were there for that, too. But they didn't actively participate. All the police have them on is being present and playing lookout.

My family's attorney said probation and a fine was the most likely outcome given the circumstances. It was their first offense on the record. I hate them both almost as much as I hate Austin. They deserve to be behind bars too, but until now ... I hadn't really considered it a possibility.

"That's not for you to worry about," Jaymin says. "But if I'm able to secure jail time for both parties, two years with the opportunity for parole, will you agree to five years for Austin?"

I consider it. Like, really consider it. If I go to trial, there's a chance Austin might serve a longer sentence, but then Gregory and Parker walk. If I take this deal, all of them have to pay for what they did to me. It's not enough, but if I'm honest with myself, I don't know that anything ever would be. They took something from me. No punishment can ever give it back. At least this way—

"I need an answer."

"Whatever I agree to now won't hold up in court," I tell her. "I can still change my mind."

"I'm aware. But I'll take a verbal confirmation now, regardless."

I chew on my bottom lip. "All three serve time behind bars," I echo her earlier statement. "Five years for Austin and I want three years for Gregory and Parker."

"I can make that happen."

We'll see.

"And I want all three going through court-ordered therapy upon release." They're already menaces to society. This way ... I don't know. Maybe other women like me will stand a chance.

Jaymin nods, her movements slow and deliberate. "I'll ensure the necessary arrangements are made."

Then ... silence as Jaymin rises from her seat without a word and slips out of the room, her heels clicking softly against the wooden floor. The sound fades, and I'm left standing in the middle of the room, frozen, unsure of what comes next.

I turn toward the window, the heavy fabric of the curtains brushing my fingertips as I pull them further back to peer out. The alley is empty, devoid of life. No cars, no people. Just the quiet hum of a distant streetlight and the shadowy outline of buildings looming in the dusk.

The seconds tick by, painfully slow. My eyes track the flickering light at the end of the street, watching it go in and out, like my breathing. Steady, but not enough to chase away the anxiety gnawing at my insides.

I press my palm flat against the cool glass, my thoughts slipping into a dull buzz. My fingers curl into a fist, pressing harder, trying to ground myself against the growing unease. *How long are they going to keep me here?*

The room feels empty without her, but not in a comforting way. It's the kind of emptiness that's full of tension, wrapping around me like a cold hand on my throat. I clench and unclench my fists, feeling the soft satin of my dress between my fingers. I try to remember my therapist's grounding exercises.

I've got this.

Finally, the sound of a phone ringing cuts through the heavy silence like a sharp blade. My body jerks at the sudden noise, adrenaline flooding my veins. I whirl around as Jaymin steps back into the room, calm and collected as always.

Her driver comes in from the opposite end of the house. His phone is pressed to his ear. He doesn't speak at first, just nods, his face unreadable.

After a pause, he lowers the phone and turns to Jaymin who stares at him with an expectant look.

"Your son is home," he tells her.

She exhales, a slow release of tension I didn't even realize she was holding. Her shoulders drop, her mask of cold indifference faltering just enough to reveal the relief beneath. "Well then," she says, her voice softer than before. "It looks like we're finished here."

Relief washes over me, mingling with exhaustion, but I can't bring myself to feel the same level of calm that she does. "Great. Can I go now?"

Jaymin retrieves my phone from her purse, holding it out to me with a small, polite smile that makes my skin crawl. "I'll have my driver drop you off."

I nod, clutching my phone tightly in my hand, the familiar weight of it somehow comforting now. "Fine."

seven

CECILIA

I FOLLOW Jaymin's driver to the car, my legs shaky but determined. The night air is cold against my skin, but it's nothing compared to the icy dread that's coiled in my stomach. The SUV looms ahead, dark and intimidating, and I swallow hard as the driver pulls the door open for me.

The ride is silent, the air inside thick with unspoken tension, so heavy it feels like I'm choking on it. My thoughts spin, tangled and knotted in the aftermath of everything.

Five years.

I can't believe I agreed to five years.

I stare out the window, watching the dark streets blur by, but I don't really see anything. The idea of him walking around, free, is almost too much to process. My fingers curl into the fabric of my dress, twisting until my knuckles turn white. Every time I think I'm safe, it's like the rug gets ripped out from under me again.

We pull up somewhere in the neighborhood where they originally picked me up, and I mutter a quick, "Thanks," before practically bolting from the car. The air hits me like a slap, cool and biting, but it does nothing to calm the storm raging inside me.

I stand on the side of the road, my breath fogging up in the chilly night as I watch the SUV disappear down the street, the taillights a dull red glow in the distance.

Reaching into my pocket, I pull out my phone. My fingers tremble as I swipe my finger over the screen. It's off again. My heart skips a beat. Did the battery die? Did Jaymin turn it off when I wasn't looking?

A few agonizing seconds pass, but then the screen lights up. Relief floods through me, so palpable I almost sag against the nearby lamppost. It's not dead. That's one positive thing going for me, at least.

Ignoring the barrage of notifications that pop up on the screen, I scroll through my contacts until I find Felix's number. He said I could call him.

I hesitate, biting my lip. Should I, though? It's late. He's probably busy.

Screw it. I need to call someone, and I'm not really coming up with a better option.

It rings once before he picks up.

"Cecilia? Is that you?" He rushes out as soon as the line connects.

The concern in his voice is like a punch to the gut, and I realize how much I've been holding my breath. "Hi. Yeah. Umm ... sorry. I know it's late. But, you said I could call—"

"Of course you can." There's noise in the background—voices, the clatter of something heavy—but Felix hushes them, muttering out, "I know, I know," before his attention returns to me. "Are you okay? Where are you?"

I rub the back of my neck, suddenly feeling self-conscious. "I'm fine," I lie, my voice sounding thin even to my own ears. "But, uh, I'm not really sure where I am. Let me check." I squint in the dim light, taking a few steps toward the corner of the street. The shadows stretch long and ominous across the pavement as I strain my eyes to make out the street name. "Hold on."

"Relax," Felix murmurs, almost to himself.

"Huh?" I glance around, confused.

"Sorry, not you," Felix says quickly. "The guys are being stupid."

Oh. "Okay, so—yeah, I'm at the corner of Priest and Boone. Is that far from you?"

The line goes quiet for a moment, and then I hear him curse under his breath, followed by a rushed conversation with someone else in the background. My stomach twists. Why does it feel like there's something more going on?

"Felix?" I say, voice wavering.

"We're on our way," he responds, his tone suddenly sharp. "Don't hang up, though. Okay?"

I frown, staring down the empty street. "Yeah. Okay." I shift on my feet, glancing nervously over my shoulder. I wasn't planning on wandering off, but the urgency in his voice makes me uneasy.

His words suddenly register. "Wait—what do you mean, 'we'? Who's with you?"

There's another muffled conversation in the background. It's obvious I've interrupted something. Guilt gnaws at me. This was a mistake. He's busy. I don't know what I was thinking. "Actually, don't worry about it," I say quickly. "I'll call a ride share. Enjoy your night—"

"DO NOT HANG UP THE PHONE."

The command is so sharp, so sudden, that I freeze mid-step. Felix has never spoken to me like that before. His voice is always easygoing, playful. This? This is something else.

"O-okay," I stammer, unsure what else to say.

He exhales, the sound rough. "Sorry. I didn't mean to snap at you. But, Cecilia ... the last few hours have been a shitshow trying to find you."

My heart skips a beat. "You were looking for me?"

"Yeah." He hesitates, and I can hear the tension in his voice. "I didn't want to tell you over the phone, but—"

I cut him off, already knowing what he's about to say. "Austin's out on bail."

The silence on the other end is heavy for a moment. Then, quietly, "You heard?"

I huff out a bitter laugh, staring up at the sky, the stars blinking coldly above me. "You could say that."

Felix's voice is softer when he speaks again. "Are you okay?"

I swallow hard, the lump in my throat making it difficult to breathe. "Yeah," I whisper, my fingers tightening around the phone. "I'm okay."

"We're less than ten minutes away. Just keep talking to me, alright? Tell me where you've been."

I hesitate. My conversation with Jaymin feels like something I need to process on my own first, something I'm not ready to share. "It's ... complicated," I hedge, my gaze flicking up and down the empty street.

"But you're safe? You're not hurt?" he asks, his voice laced with concern.

"I'm not hurt," I assure him. "Just ... a little shaken up."

We fall into small talk, the minutes ticking by as I keep my eyes on the dark road. I'm glad Felix made me stay on the phone. Being out here, alone, in the dark, sends a chill creeping up my spine. Every gust of wind, every shadow feels like it's hiding something. Someone.

A pair of headlights cuts through the night, the beams growing brighter as they approach. My heart picks up, and I squint, trying to make out the car.

"That's us," Felix says through the phone. "I see you. We're pulling up now."

We both end the call as his car pulls to a stop in front of me. The passenger door flies open before the car even comes to a full stop, and Felix curses as Gabriel barrels out, heading straight for me.

"Cecilia!" Gabriel's voice is hoarse, desperate. Before I can even process what's happening, he has me wrapped in his arms, my feet lifting me off the ground like he can't bear the distance.

His body is warm, solid, and I cling to him without hesitation. My heart is pounding in my chest, and I squeeze him tight. His breathing is ragged as he buries his face in my neck, and I feel the soft tremble in his shoulders.

"Fuck, I was so worried," he breathes, his lips brushing the sensitive skin of my throat. His hold on me is tight, like he's afraid I'll disappear if he loosens his grip.

I don't understand what's happening. He was so angry earlier. But right now, all I feel is his desperation, his need to be close to me.

I don't have time to think, to question. My body reacts to his without thought, my arms winding tighter around his neck, holding him like he's the only thing keeping me grounded.

He sets me back on my feet, but his hands never leave me, cupping my face, his forehead pressed against mine. "I thought I lost you," he whispers, his breath warm and ragged against my skin.

I blink, confusion swirling inside me. "I thought you were mad—"

He cuts me off with his mouth, crashing into mine with a fierceness that steals my breath. For a split second, I forget everything—where I am, what I was going to say—and kiss him back, hard. His lips are demanding, his kiss rough and desperate, and I can feel the raw emotion behind it.

But then reality slams into me.

"Wait," I gasp, pulling back, but Gabriel doesn't let go. His lips press to my cheek, my temple, trailing warmth and fire wherever they touch.

"Gabriel—"

"It's okay," he murmurs against my skin. "I've got you. I'm here."

But that's not what I mean. I push against his chest, confusion and anger swirling inside me, mixing into a chaotic mess. "I can't do this," I whisper, more to myself than to him, but I push harder.

His arms drop, uncertainty flickering in his eyes as I step back, the space between us suddenly too much and not enough at the same time.

"What's wrong?" he asks, his voice cracking slightly.

I shake my head, tears pricking the backs of my eyes. "Where is this coming from?" My voice is shaky, my chest tightening with emotions I don't understand. "You were furious with me a few hours ago. You wouldn't even talk to me. What's changed?"

His face softens, and he steps closer again, his hand reaching for mine. "I was an idiot," he admits, his voice rough with regret. "I thought I lost you, Cecilia." His words are a whisper, meant only for me. "When I found out Holt got out and I couldn't find you ... I thought ... I can't even say it out loud."

I look into his eyes, seeing the truth there. The fear. The vulnerability. He pulls me close again, pressing my head to his chest. His heart races beneath my ear, pounding hard and fast.

"Fuck, I hope you can forgive me," he whispers into my hair, his voice broken. "I *need* you to forgive me. I was out of line. I wasn't—" he chokes out his words. "I wasn't thinking straight."

"There's nothing to forgive," I whisper back, but the words feel heavy, weighed down by all the emotions swirling inside me.

Gabriel's arms tighten around me, his body a shield against the world, but I can feel the weight of his guilt, the tension radiating from him. His chest rises and falls in uneven breaths, and I close my eyes, sinking deeper into his warmth, even though I know I shouldn't. Not like this.

"You don't have to lie to me," he says, his voice raw, vibrating through his chest. "I fucked up. You needed me, and I wasn't there for you. But I'm going to fix this. I won't let you down again, I swear."

I pull back just enough to look up at him, the shadows of the streetlights casting lines across his face, making him look both softer and harder all at once. His honey-brown eyes search mine, desperate for something, and I know he's looking for forgiveness, but it's more than that. He needs me to trust him again. To believe he can protect me, even when everything feels out of control.

But trust? That's not something you can fix with a few words and a desperate kiss.

"I'm not lying," I say, my voice small, my chest tightening. "I'm just ... tired, Gabriel. I'm really freaking tired."

He lifts his hand, brushing a strand of hair from my face, the touch so gentle, so reverent, it makes my throat burn. "I know, baby. I know you are." His voice drops lower, rougher. "Come home with me."

I blink up at him, heart stuttering in my chest. "What?"

"Just for tonight," he murmurs, his forehead pressing against mine again, his breath warm against my lips. "You're exhausted, and I'm losing my fucking mind. I just need to know you're okay. I need to keep you close. For my own sanity."

I close my eyes, my resolve crumbling with every word he speaks. I *should* say no. I should push him away, tell him we need space, that this isn't the answer. But my body betrays me, leaning into him, craving the safety his arms promise.

After everything that's happened tonight, there's nowhere else I'd feel safe. No one else I'd trust to keep me grounded.

"It's a bad idea," I whisper, the words barely audible as I rest my head back against his chest. His heart is still pounding, matching the frantic rhythm of my own.

"Then why does it feel like the only option?" he asks softly, his lips brushing my temple.

A shiver runs down my spine, and I nod, unable to argue with the truth in his words. Because it *does* feel like the only option. Even if it's temporary. Even if I know we're walking a dangerous line.

Gabriel's the only one I want near me right now.

"Okay," I whisper, almost to myself. "Just for tonight."

His arms tighten, and I can feel the tension leave his body, like he was holding his breath, waiting for me to pull away. "Thank you." His voice is thick with relief.

Without another word, Gabriel takes my hand and leads me to the car. His touch is firm but gentle, his thumb brushing over my knuckles as if he's afraid I'll disappear if he lets go. Felix sits in the front seat, his gaze flicking between us as we slide into the back.

"Everything good?" Felix asks, his tone cautious, but filled with an unspoken understanding.

Gabriel nods, pulling me into his side the moment we're both seated. "Yeah. We're good."

Felix doesn't ask any more questions, just throws the car into drive and heads for the soccer house. I lean into Gabriel, letting his warmth seep into me, the steady rhythm of his breathing a balm to my frayed nerves. His arm stays wrapped around me the entire ride, his fingers tracing light patterns on my arm.

When we pull up to the house, Gabriel doesn't waste a second. He opens the door and helps me out, his hand never leaving mine as he guides me inside. The familiar smell of him—cologne and something distinctly *Gabriel*—soothes me, keeps me from falling apart.

The house is quiet, the lights dim, and there's an eerie sense of calm as we walk through the door. It feels surreal, like this moment isn't supposed to exist. Like we're suspended in time, just the two of us, trying to navigate through all the wreckage of tonight.

"You need anything? Water? Something to eat?"

I shake my head. "No. I'm okay."

Julio and Atticus, with Deacon only a few steps behind them, step into the room having come from deeper within the house.

"Everything good?" Julio asks, taking in the three of us.

"All good," Felix says, but some other form of silent communication passes between them.

"We're going to head upstairs. We'll talk more in the morning," Gabriel tells them.

Julio frowns but doesn't object as Gabriel tugs on my hand, encouraging me to follow him.

"Goodnight," I tell the guys.

"Goodnight," a chorus of voices responds.

"C'mon," Gabriel murmurs, his voice soft, but insistent, as he leads me up the stairs and into his room. It's dimly lit, the moonlight filtering through the blinds, casting soft shadows across the bed. His space is always so clean, so organized, and yet right now, it feels like the safest mess I could ever step into.

I sit on the edge of the bed, running my fingers through my hair, trying to shake off the weight of the day, but it clings to me like a second skin.

Gabriel crouches in front of me, his warm hands on my bare knees, his eyes searching mine with so much intensity it makes my chest ache. "You okay?"

"I will be," I whisper. "I just ... need a minute."

He nods, his thumb brushing over my skin again, sending shivers racing up my spine. "Take all the time you need. I'm not going anywhere."

I believe him.

Seconds pass, turning into minutes, both of us too afraid to break the silence. Whatever this is, whatever moment of peace we've found together, it feels fragile, and I don't want to be the one to shatter it.

"You know you can talk to me," he murmurs.

"Do you want to talk about the wedding?" I counter.

His lips press into a thin line, and he shakes his head no.

"I don't want to talk about tonight, either."

"We need to," he tells me.

"After you."

His brows pull together, and his expression darkens. I can tell he doesn't like my response.

"Tomorrow?"

I consider it. "Okay," I tell him. "We can talk about all of the hard stuff tomorrow."

eight
GABRIEL

IT TAKES everything in me to walk away from her. My muscles scream to stay, to pull her closer, but I know if I don't step back now, I'll push her for something she's not ready to give. So I force myself to stand. My chest feels tight, every inch of me resisting the distance, but I manage to mutter, "I'll be right back," and walk away.

Grabbing a pair of sweats from my dresser, I head into the bathroom and get changed for the night, leaving my chest bare. The mirror above the sink catches my reflection, and I pause, bracing my hands against the counter as I take in the strain lining my face. My jaw clenches. My eyes are rimmed with exhaustion, shadows dark beneath them. Fuck. It feels like I've aged a decade in the span of a few hours.

I run a hand through my hair, trying to calm the storm brewing inside me, but it doesn't help.

Flicking off the light, I return to my room.

She's still on the bed where I left her, knees drawn up, her body small against the backdrop of my space.

I grab a shirt from my closet, setting it beside her before crouching down in front of her, close enough to feel the heat radiating off her body.

"Do you want to get ready for bed?" I ask softly, my voice thick with emotion I'm barely holding back.

She exhales, and the soft brush of her breath against my skin sends shivers through me. Her eyes travel down my bare chest, and I swallow hard, trying to tamp down the desire that's rising fast and relentless inside me.

Her gaze is appreciative—hell, it's more than that. It's hungry. The kind of look that makes my body respond before my mind can stop it.

She reaches out, her fingers grazing my skin, barely touching, but enough to ignite the need that's been simmering just beneath the surface. It's almost too much. The smell of her, the softness of her touch—it's intoxicating, and I'm quickly losing control.

But I can't. I kissed her once tonight, and she pulled away. I'm not about to fuck this up by moving too fast. I have to hold back. *For her.*

Then she leans forward, her lips brushing against my chest, so soft it feels like fire licking up my spine. I shudder. She pulls back just enough for our eyes to meet, and the air thickens between us, heavy and electric. Then she says the last thing I expect to hear right now.

"I know it's not fair, and it's really fucked up of me to even suggest this, but ... I ... could we ..." Her voice trails off, uncertainty lacing her words, but her dark brown eyes lock on mine, pleading, searching.

I know what she's asking. At least, I hope I do. And fuck, if she wants this—needs this—I'm powerless to say no.

She presses her lips to my collarbone, and I suck in a breath, my control slipping further away as her hands explore the planes of my chest. My muscles tense beneath her touch, my hands gripping her thighs, pulling her closer, almost without thinking. This is dangerous. She's been through something tonight, something big, and I don't know the details yet. But I can't deny her. I never could.

My hands slide lower, gripping beneath her thighs as I spread them wider, positioning myself between her legs. Her warmth draws me in, my need for her wrapping tighter around my chest.

"You're sure?" I ask, my lips hovering just inches from hers, giving her one last chance to pull away.

"Yes." Her voice is a breathy whisper, her need echoing mine.

I'm going to hell for this.

I inch closer, watching for any sign of hesitation, but she meets me halfway, her lips crashing into mine. The kiss starts slow, soft, but quickly turns into something more—something desperate and hungry. Her hands are in my hair, pulling me closer, and I lose myself in her.

"Cecilia," I groan against her mouth, my hands wandering over her body, feeling the soft curves, the heat radiating off her skin. I grip the backs of her thighs, lifting her higher onto the bed.

She gasps, arching beneath me as I settle my weight between her legs, her body molding to mine like she was made for me.

Her fingers tangle in my hair, tugging me closer. She deepens the kiss, and I can't think straight. All I know is that I need more of her. I slide my hand beneath the hem of her dress, fingers grazing the smooth skin just beneath her panties.

"Tell me what you need," I demand, my voice rough, almost desperate.

"More," she breathes, her body arching into mine, begging for the release I know she craves.

I press my erection against her center, rocking into her heat. My control is hanging by a thread. "This?" I ask, teasing, pushing her to the edge with nothing but words.

She shakes her head, breath coming in short, shallow pants. "Please," she whispers, her hips rising to meet mine, her body trembling beneath me. "I need—"

"Tell me," I growl, lips brushing along her neck before I bite down, hard enough to leave a mark. Her sharp gasp sends a thrill through me, her nails digging into my back.

"Gabriel!" she cries, and fuck, the way she says my name ... it wrecks me.

"Words, baby. I need to hear the words." I can't—won't—go further without them. She's not thinking clearly tonight. Her emotions are running too high. But I need to know she wants this as much as I do.

"I need you," she finally says, her voice thick with desire, shattering any doubt.

"I'm right here," I murmur, my lips brushing hers again. "Yours for the taking."

Her eyes burn with lust as she pushes herself up on her elbows, gaze trailing down my body. She licks her lips, and I nearly lose it. My control is slipping, but I want her to make a move.

Cecilia's fingers trail down my chest, lingering over the hard ridges of my abdomen. I suck in a sharp breath, waiting, anticipation tightening every muscle in my body. Her hand dips lower, grazing the waistband of my sweats, and I hold my breath.

"Touch me," I whisper, my voice raw. "There's nothing in this world I want more."

Emboldened, she slips her hand beneath the fabric, her fingers wrapping around my length. A groan escapes my lips, hips thrusting into her fist. "Fuck," I mutter, my voice strangled. "Take me out."

With trembling hands, Cecilia pulls my cock free, her thumb brushing over the tip. I grit my teeth, my hips moving instinctively in her hand. "Jesus." I could come just like this. Just from the warmth of her hand.

Her touch is tentative at first, but she quickly finds her rhythm, her hand moving in slow, torturous strokes. "Yes," I groan, my voice hoarse with need. "Tighter, baby. Just like that."

Her gaze locks with mine, dark and filled with desire. "I want you inside me," she breathes, her voice a sultry whisper that sends a shiver down my spine.

Without another word, I kick off my sweats and tear her clothes from her body, leaving her completely bare. She's breathtaking, every inch of her flushed and ready for me. I lower my mouth to her breast, sucking and nipping at the sensitive peaks of her nipples until she's writhing beneath me. Her moans are a symphony of pleasure I can't get enough of.

"Are you wet for me?" I ask, sliding my fingers down to her core, feeling the slickness between her thighs.

"Yes," she gasps, her hips lifting off the bed, chasing my fingers as they retreat. "Please, Gabriel."

The need to bury myself inside her is overwhelming, but I hold back. Not yet. I press two fingers into her, feeling her stretch around me, her body quivering beneath my touch.

"Fuck, you're soaked," I murmur, pumping my fingers inside her. I watch her face as she races toward release, her breaths coming faster, her body trembling.

She gasps, her fingers digging into the sheets. "Right there," she cries, her voice strained. "Don't stop."

"Never," I whisper, pressing my thumb to her clit. I circle it slowly, driving her higher and higher. Her body arches off the bed, and I know she's close. A fine sheen of sweat sticking to her skin.

When she finally falls apart, it's like watching something divine. She shatters beneath me, her body clenching around my fingers as I watch her, every muscle tightening, her lips parted in a breathless cry. "Gabriel!"

Fuck, hearing my name on her lips as she comes is enough to make me lose it.

I barely give her a moment to recover before I line myself up with her entrance. "Are you ready for me?" I ask, my voice thick with need.

She whines, a desperate sound that has me ready to give her anything she wants. My body is on fire, every inch of me straining with the need to be inside her, to lose myself in her heat. But I won't rush this. Not tonight. Not with her like this.

"Words, baby," I remind her. My fingers brush her sweat dampened hair away from her face as I keep my voice low and controlled, though I'm anything but.

"Yes," she breathes. "Please, Gabriel. Make me forget."

Her words gut me, the plea in her voice slicing through my chest. I know what she's asking—what she needs—and it kills me that I don't have all the answers, that I can't fix whatever it is that's haunting her right now. We'll come back to that tomorrow. But right now, I can give her this.

Slowly, I push inside her, inch by torturous inch. Her slick heat wraps around me like a vice. My control is hanging by a thread, my jaw clenched so tight it hurts. "Jesus," I hiss, fighting to keep it together as her body takes me in.

She curses softly, her spine curving off the bed, her legs wrapping tighter around my waist as I bury myself to the hilt. I pause, giving her a moment to adjust, to feel every inch of me inside her, but fuck—it takes everything I have not to move, not to come right here and now after only one thrust.

"Gabriel," she whispers, her voice soft, breathless, her hands gripping my shoulders like I'm the only thing anchoring her to the earth. "Please."

I press my forehead to hers, my breaths coming in ragged pants as I start to move, slowly at first, rocking into her with long, deep strokes. Her breath hitches every time I thrust inside her, her body trembling beneath me as she rises to meet every push of my hips. The way she fits around me, so tight, so perfect—it's heaven and hell all at once.

"Fuck, you feel so good," I groan, my hands gripping her hips, guiding her against me, driving deeper with every thrust. The tension between us builds, thick and suffocating, but I can't stop. Won't stop. Not when she feels like this, like she was made for me.

Her nails rake down my back, her breaths coming faster, each one catching in her throat as I pick up the pace, thrusting harder, faster. I can feel her unraveling beneath me, her body quaking, her moans growing louder, more desperate.

"Faster," she pleads, her voice breaking. "Please, Gabriel, faster."

I lose the last of my control, driving into her with a force that has the bed shaking beneath us, her cries echoing off the walls. Every thrust sends her higher, closer to the edge, and fuck, I want to see her fall apart again. I want to feel her come undone around me.

"Gabriel!" she cries, her body tensing, her muscles clenching tight around my cock as she shatters. Her orgasm hits hard, her back arching off the bed as her lips part in a silent scream. She's trembling, her entire body shaking with the force of it, and it's enough to send me over the edge.

I bury myself deep, my fingers digging into her hips as my own release slams into me, my vision going white as I spill inside her. Her name falls from my lips in a ragged groan, my body collapsing against hers as the aftershocks roll through me.

For a long moment, neither of us moves, our breaths coming in heavy, uneven gasps. I press my forehead to her shoulder, my body still trembling from the intensity of it all. She's warm beneath me, soft, her skin slick with sweat and sex, and I don't ever want to move. Don't ever want to let her go.

Finally, I shift, careful not to crush her as I roll to my side, pulling her with me. She curls into my chest, her breathing slowly evening out, her fingers tracing lazy patterns over my skin. I kiss the top of her head, pressing my lips to her hair as I hold her close.

"Thank you," she whispers, her voice so soft I almost don't hear it.

I close my eyes, my chest tightening at the sound of her words. I don't know what she's thanking me for. For not pushing her? For giving her what she needed tonight?

"We'll talk in the morning," I murmur, my lips brushing her forehead.

She mumbles something incoherent, already half-asleep, and snuggles deeper into my arms. I hold her tighter, my heart racing with too many emotions to name. I know we have things to work out, things to say, but for now, this—her in my arms, safe and warm—is enough.

The steady rhythm of her breathing is the only sound in the room, and I try to let it calm the storm still raging inside me. But sleep doesn't come. Not for me. My mind is too full—of her, of the panic I felt tonight, of everything I don't know but need to. I stare up at the ceiling, my arms wrapped tight around her, my thoughts spinning.

Austin Holt is out there, and I don't know what went down tonight, but I know one thing—I won't let anything, or anyone, hurt her again.

I press another kiss to her hair, holding her close as I finally close my eyes, letting the warmth of her body pull me under. Having her here like this feels right.

It feels like home.

nine

GABRIEL

SUNLIGHT FILTERS INTO THE ROOM, dragging with it memories of last night. I reach out blindly, searching for the warmth of Cecilia's body. But I find nothing but cold sheets. My heart lurches, eyes snapping open. Where the hell is she?

Throwing the covers back, I swing my legs over the edge of the bed, feet hitting the hardwood floor with a dull thud. The knot in my stomach tightens as I take in the empty room. She wouldn't just leave. Right?

I yank on my discarded sweatpants, movements sharp, leaving my chest bare as I scan the clock—6:30 AM. Too early for anyone else in the house to be awake. The silence hangs heavy, and my pulse picks up.

I pause at the bathroom door, pressing my ear against it. Nothing. The quiet gnaws at me. I push the door open, only to find emptiness staring back at me. The space feels hollow, mocking me.

Fuck.

She doesn't have her Jeep. She couldn't have gone far. Panic starts to creep in, clawing at my chest. I jog downstairs, first checking the living room. Empty. My eyes flick to the front door, but something pulls me toward the kitchen.

And then I see her.

Cecilia, standing at the counter, her back to me. Her hair is a mess from sleep, dark strands tangled over her shoulders, and she's wearing my shirt. Only my shirt. It hangs loose, mid-thigh, giving me a glimpse of her bare skin as she reaches up for the coffee canister.

Fuck me.

I stop in the doorway, adjusting myself because just looking at her undoes me. The knot of worry loosens, replaced by something primal. My heart pounds, and for a second, all I can do is stare. Everything about her—the way my shirt clings to her curves, her skin glowing in the soft morning light—grips me tight.

I step into the kitchen, clearing my throat to make my presence known. "Here," I say, moving behind her and turning the coffee pot on, my fingers brushing hers as she pours the grounds.

She stiffens at my touch, her body tensing—a wall going up. "Thanks," she mutters, brushing her hair back, revealing tired, red-rimmed eyes. She looks ... wrecked.

I frown, stepping closer, the warmth of her body pulling me in like gravity. The soft brush of her skin against my chest, the way her scent—coconut with a hint of vanilla—wraps around me is intoxicating. It tightens my chest, makes me crave more.

"Did you sleep okay?" I ask, reaching up for the mugs, but my eyes stay on her, watching every small movement. It's like the air in the room shifts between us. Too much, too soon? Or not enough? Fuck if I know anymore.

Her fingers trace the counter, avoiding my gaze. "Not really," she whispers, the words barely there.

My heart sinks. I want to pull her into my arms, but something in her posture stops me. She's distant, closed off, and the ache in my chest intensifies.

"How come?" I ask, my voice quieter than I intended. The need to fix this, to fix her, is overwhelming, but I can't do that unless she lets me in.

She sighs, her eyes drifting to the window. "I had a lot on my mind."

No surprise there. Holt getting out, the way she disappeared last night—there's a lot going on. But knowing that doesn't ease the knot in my stomach.

"About last night ..." I trail off, searching her face for any sign she's ready to talk, but she shakes her head, cutting me off.

"Not yet," she mumbles, her voice hesitant. "But ..." Her gaze flickers to mine for a brief moment before darting away again. "We do need to talk. About other things."

That sends a chill down my spine. Nothing good ever comes from *we need to talk*. I swallow, trying to keep my voice steady. "Like?"

Cecilia hesitates, her shoulders slumping as she grips the edge of the counter. "Last night was ..." She pauses, eyes briefly meeting mine.

79

"It was great," I say, stepping into her space, needing to close the distance. I brush a lock of her hair behind her ear, tilting her chin up. "It was perfect." Her wide brown eyes lock with mine, and for a second, I think I've gotten through to her.

But then she blushes, that pretty shade of pink staining her cheeks, and she shakes her head. "Yeah, but ... what does it mean?"

It fucking means everything. I keep my face neutral. Does she want it to mean something? Because it means everything to me.

But if I say that, if I tell her it means we're good, back on solid ground, and that she owns my fucking heart, will she freak out and push me away?

Fuck. I don't want to brush it off as a one-night thing. We're so far past that. But what's the right answer here?

"What do you want it to mean?" My voice is calm, though every muscle in my body is taut.

Cecilia inhales sharply and takes a small step back. I can see her walls going up. She's retreating again, pulling away.

Fuck. Fuck. Fuck.

What did I say wrong?

"I don't want to keep doing this," she says, her voice a little stronger now, but there's an edge to it. "Every time we get close, something happens. We mess it up."

Her words gut me, but I keep my face steady. She's been through hell, and I don't want to add to her burden. But god, I want to shake her and tell her I can't go backwards. That I need her in my life—fully, completely. But what if pushing her sends her running? What if I mess this up before it even begins?

I feel the shift. She's slipping, distancing herself. Before I can respond, she steps back completely, crossing her arms over her chest like a shield.

"We're stuck in this loop," she continues, pacing a few steps toward the sink. "I don't know how to break it. And I don't know if I'm strong enough to try right now."

Her words cut deeper than I expected. I can practically feel my chest squeezing tighter. She's scared, running like she always does when things get complicated.

"So what are you saying?" My voice is tense, frustration leaking through.

"I don't know." She turns to face me, her voice shaking. "I don't know what I'm saying, Gabriel. I just know that ... last night ..." She holds her arms tighter around herself, like she's trying to build a barrier between us. "I don't know where we stand and not knowing, it's messing me all up inside."

My stomach twists painfully. "I don't know where we stand, either," I tell her.

What I don't say is that I know exactly where I want us to be standing. That she's my girl. The only place she belongs is by my side, but for some goddamn reason, I can't get the words out.

Because what if she doesn't want to hear it?

She stares out the window, sunlight casting her in a soft glow. It makes her look almost untouchable. Several seconds pass in silence, and I fight the urge to fill it.

When she finally turns my way, her expression is tired but resolute.

"I need to know what this is," she says, but her voice wavers. "I don't know if I'm ready for—"she motions the space between us, "—whatever this is. But I do know that I need boundaries and labels and just ... I need to know, Gabriel. I need to know what you want from me? Where you see this going if it's going anywhere at all? I just need to know."

I step forward, closing the distance between us, my hands itching to pull her close. Every instinct screams at me to hold her. "It's whatever you want it to be," I tell her, my voice soft but firm. "Whatever you're ready for. That's what this is. It's you and me, and yeah, baby, we're a thing. But we're moving at your pace. This is all on your timeline, okay? I'm not going to rush you, but I'm here. I'm in this."

Her lip trembles, and for a second, I think she'll let me in. But then she steps back, crossing her arms again. The warmth between us fades as quickly as it came.

"My life is a mess right now, Gabriel. I can't tell up from down, and with the trial stuff coming up ... I don't see things settling down anytime soon."

A wave of frustration builds in my chest, crawling beneath my skin. "I know. But, you're not in this alone. All you have to do is let me in."

She stays silent for a beat, the smell of coffee filling the air, her eyes flicking between mine as if trying to decide how much to let me see.

"It's just really bad timing," she says, almost pleading.

I nod, jaw clenched, heart sinking. "Right." The word tastes bitter, but I swallow it down.

The coffee machine beeps, breaking the tension. I pour us both a cup, watching as she adds a splash of creamer. She takes a tentative sip, a small smile passing over her lips.

"So, friends?" I ask, raising a brow, trying to keep things light. Even though it fucking kills me to say it. My chest tightens at the thought, but if that's what she needs, I'll take it.

Her smile falters, her eyes dimming.

Shit. Did I read that wrong?

"If you want that, I mean." My voice wavers, panic bubbling up. Fuck. I sound like such a simp but I can't find it in myself to care. "I know you have a lot on your plate, but I'm here," I reiterate. "For whatever you need. You can lean on me."

She shakes her head, her lip trembling again. "Yeah," she stammers. "Friends is fine. Great even."

Bullshit.

If friends was fine she wouldn't look like she was two seconds away from crying. My heart swells in my chest. I hate seeing my girl upset, but does that mean she wants more? That she wants me?

I take her mug from her hands, setting it aside before grabbing her chin gently, forcing her to look at me. "What is it, baby?"

Her eyes drop, and she tries to pull away, but I'm not letting her. I pull her closer until her chest is flush against mine.

"None of this works if we lie to each other."

She buries her face in my chest, and I wrap my arms around her, resting my chin on top of her head. Her body trembles against me, and my heart feels like it's breaking for her. "I thought ... I thought you'd want to give things a real shot. I know I already said things are a mess. And I know my problems don't need to be yours. Right now is the worst possible time to start a relationship. Trust me, I know. And I get that it's a lot to ask."

Her words sink in like a slap upside the head and I cut her off mid ramble. "You're joking, right?"

Her brows furrow, and she hastily wipes at her eyes with the backs of her hands. "Sorry. God. I'm such a mess. I don't know what I was thinking. Just ignore me, okay? Friends is great. It's more than I—"

"Cecilia, we're getting our wires crossed." I tilt her chin toward me again, needing her to hear me. "You said your life was a mess. I thought that meant you weren't ready for a relationship."

"It is a mess," she stammers, her voice shaky. "And I'm not 100% ready. Not in the 'lets be responsible and jump in feet first' kind of way. I think I'm more of the 'let's go head first and hope for the best' sort of way. But that's okay, right? Life is messy. We have ups and downs but umm ... I'm not really sure where I'm going with all that but—" Her watery smile meets mine.

"Tell me what you want," I say, needing to hear the words. "I'm all in, baby. Friends, dating, hell, marriage—you name it. Whatever you want, I'm in. Just tell me what you want and it's yours."

Her eyes widen, vulnerability shining through. She looks at me like I'm offering her the world.

"You're serious?"

"As a heart attack." I brush a tear from her cheek. "But I'm gonna need you to talk to me. I'm not a mind reader, and we've got a history of getting our wires crossed."

Her lip quivers. "I don't deserve you."

I pull her tight against me, my hands gripping her waist. "You deserve everything, Cecilia. Fucking everything."

She clings to me for a long moment, then pulls back just slightly. "I want a fresh start," she says softly. "Like, really start over. Date each other. But slow. I think I need slow with everything going on, but I want to give us a try."

I nod, my heart slamming against my ribs. "We'll take it as slow as you need. I'm not going anywhere."

She exhales, the tension melting from her shoulders. "And ... maybe no sex for a while," she adds quickly. "I just ... I want to make sure we're building something real, you know?"

The no-sex part stings a little, but I get it. "If that's what you want, then that's what we'll do."

Her smile returns, and this time it feels real. "Really?"

"Really." I cup her cheek, brushing my thumb across her skin. "I'm in this for the long haul."

"Thank you," she whispers, resting her head against my chest.

We stand there, wrapped up in each other, the smell of coffee and the warmth of her body grounding me like a blanket. For the first time in a long time, it feels like we're on the same page. Like we actually have a shot at making this work.

"I'll take you out," I murmur into her hair. "Proper dates. Dinner, movies, whatever you want."

She chuckles softly, the sound vibrating through my chest. "I'd like that."

"Good," I say, pressing a kiss to her forehead. "Because I've got a lot of making up to do, and I plan on spoiling you rotten."

Her laugh is soft and genuine, and it's the best sound I've heard in weeks. "I'm looking forward to it," she says, her fingers tracing the edge of my jaw.

We're interrupted by the sound of shuffling feet, and we both glance toward the doorway to find my roommates lingering awkwardly.

"Uh, hey," Atticus rubs the back of his neck, his face a little red. "We didn't want to interrupt, but ..."

Felix pushes his way into the room, Julio right behind him. "But we're starving," Felix says. "And we need caffeine before practice."

I chuckle, shaking my head. It's so typical of them that I can't help but grin. "Alright, alright. Pancakes, bacon, and eggs, coming right up." I turn to Cecilia. "You up for it?"

She grins, nodding. "Absolutely."

ten

GABRIEL

THE GUYS SETTLE into the space, banter flying, jokes easy and sharp. Cecilia and I work side by side, laughing and teasing like old times. As we move around the kitchen, the smell of fresh coffee and sizzling bacon filling the air, a sense of normalcy settles over us. The kind of normal that used to feel so far away.

The ease of it all tugs at something deep inside me, making it feel like we've stepped into a kind of comfortable rhythm. It's chaotic, but it feels right. Like maybe, just maybe, this thing between us has a real chance.

"You know," Deacon says, his voice casual as he leans against the counter, "if this whole soccer thing doesn't work out, you could always open a café."

I snort. "I'll keep that in mind."

Cecilia chuckles beside me, shooting me a playful look. The warmth in her gaze settles the leftover tension from earlier, and

I can't help but smile back. It feels like we're getting there—slowly, but we're getting there.

"Here, let me get that," I say, reaching to help her pour the batter onto the griddle. Our hands brush, and I let my fingers linger just for a second longer than necessary. She grins, and for a moment, everything feels easy.

The guys fall into conversation again, laughter bouncing off the walls. It's the kind of noise that drowns out all the heavy shit from the last few weeks. I want to hold onto it—to us—right here.

As we finish eating, I check the time. "We should get going," I say, standing up and gathering the plates. "Coach is already going to make us run the gauntlet. No need to piss him off even more by being late."

Cecilia stands too, and I catch her hand, squeezing gently. "I'll drop you off at home," I tell her.

She nods, her fingers tightening around mine. "Yeah, okay."

I dip down for a quick kiss, our lips brushing softly before I remember the guys are here. It's a small moment, but it feels like a promise—one I want to keep.

We make quick work of cleaning up the kitchen, and before long, we're outside, the cool morning air hitting my skin. I keep Cecilia close as we walk to the car, my hand wrapped around hers.

"We'll meet you there," Deacon calls from across the driveway, climbing into Atticus's car while the rest of us pile into Julio's.

Felix claims the front seat, leaving me and Cecilia in the back. The drive to her house is filled with easy banter. Julio and Felix tease me about everything from my cooking skills to my new position as striker.

When we pull up in front of her place, I jog around to open her door. "I'll call you later, okay?" I murmur, brushing my thumb across her cheek.

She leans in, and I meet her halfway as she presses a soft kiss to my lips. "See you later."

As soon as we're back on the road, Felix twists in his seat, a sly grin spreading across his face. "So, you and Cecilia ... Is this official? Do we have labels or what?"

Julio snorts, smacking Felix on the back of the head without taking his eyes off the road. "Give him a break, man. A lot of shit's gone down in the last twenty-four hours. Gabe's got some things to figure out first."

I meet Felix's gaze head-on. "We're taking it slow, but yeah. We're together."

Felix grins wider. "Good to hear, bro. But from what we all heard last night ..." He wiggles his brows. The guys laugh, the mood light.

My face heats, my jaw clenching. A familiar flash of protectiveness surges. "Watch it, Felix." My voice comes out in a low growl.

Julio chuckles, shaking his head. "You know Felix—he's got zero chill."

"Yeah, relax," Felix says, his grin not fading. "Happy looks good on you."

"Thanks," I mutter, finally relaxing as their teasing softens into something more familiar. It feels good to talk about her like this —like we're solid, like she's really mine.

When we arrive at the field, the mood shifts instantly. The lightness of the drive evaporates. Coach is already there, a stern look etched on his face. His arms are crossed over his chest, and it's clear from the set of his jaw that today's practice isn't going to be fun.

"Remember how much you love the game," Julio mutters as we all climb out of the car and head for the field. "We're all going to need that reminder today."

———

THE SECOND I STEP ONTO THE FIELD—THE SHARP SCENT OF freshly cut grass fills my lungs—I know Coach isn't fucking around. The air is thick with tension, hanging over us like a storm ready to break.

We lost good players when Holt was kicked off the team, and the guys who walked out with him left us with massive gaps in the lineup. Now, Coach is testing us, shuffling positions, trying to see who can step up and who's going to crack under pressure.

Practice starts hard. The slap of the ball echoes in the air, the thud of feet pounding the turf steady like a heartbeat. It's a grind from the first whistle—drills that make you feel like you're drowning, testing our endurance and forcing us to work together under fire. Sweat drips down my back, soaking into the waistband of my shorts. The sun beats down mercilessly, but there's no time to think about it. No time for anything but the game.

Trial by fucking fire, that's what this is.

I'm back in my new position as striker, and Deacon's my attacking midfielder. Thank god we're in sync because everything else is chaos.

We move as one, the ball an extension of us—his pass sharp, my feet quick. The way the field opens up in front of us feels like something out of a dream. We tear down the field, the roar of our coach and the excited cheer from Jameia—our assistant coach—fade into the background. Our rhythm clicks into place, the thud of the ball against my cleats a steady rhythm, and for a second, there's hope.

Maybe we've got a shot at next week's game after all.

But the freshmen? Fuck. They're struggling. Their movements are jerky, uncoordinated, hesitation etched into every step. They're not aggressive enough, too uncertain when it comes to making plays. You can see the worry in their eyes—the fear of screwing up, of letting the team down. Every fumble sends a ripple of frustration through the field, and each time they hesitate, Coach's whistle cuts through the air like a blade.

"Cones!" Coach's voice is sharp, like the crack of a whip. He sends us to run gassers—fucking sprints that burn like fire, our lungs screaming for air, muscles quivering with every step. The grass beneath my cleats feels heavier with each pass, and damn if gassers aren't the worst. Who the fuck came up with them for soccer? Sweat runs down my face, stinging my eyes, and I blink it away, focusing on the next sprint.

My legs burn, my lungs feel like they're on fire, and I can't help but grit my teeth every time Coach yells at us to do another round. The taste of salt from the sweat on my lips makes me want to spit, but there's no time for that. Two freshmen and a sophomore have already puked on the touchlines, but no one's tapping out. Pride's the only thing keeping the rest of us going.

The sound of cleats pounding the turf becomes the soundtrack to our misery, especially Felix, who looks like he's about to keel over any second.

"You doing okay?" I ask Deacon as we sprint down the field. My breath is labored, muscles burning like they're about to tear.

"Peachy," he says, not even winded. Fucker doesn't seem out of breath. "You get used to two-a-days," he tells me, his voice almost casual. "Still fucking sucks. But I've got the endurance for stuff like this."

Lucky him. I grit my teeth, forcing my body to keep moving. My muscles scream for relief, but I push through, my focus narrowing on Deacon as we set up for another play. I glance at the field, the heat shimmering in the distance, and block everything out but the ball at my feet and the next goal in sight.

Coach blows the whistle, and I'm off, weaving through defenders, the ball glued to my feet. My heart pounds against my ribs, each beat like a war drum, adrenaline surging through my veins. Deacon's right there with me, our connection seamless, like we're reading each other's minds. The field opens up, and we push forward, cutting through the chaos like a blade.

Our offense might be on point, but defense? It's a fucking disaster. Shaky as hell, and if we don't lock it down, it won't matter how many goals we score next week.

Another fuck-up, and Coach's whistle shrieks again. The sound pierces the air, and I clench my jaw, bracing for the order.

"Gassers! Now!"

Dammit. My legs feel like they're made of lead, but I jog back to the cones, steeling myself for another round. Every breath feels like fire in my chest, but I push past it. There's no other option. I don't complain, though. None of us do. Complaining only makes it worse. The field blurs slightly, the sun relentless overhead, but we keep moving, pushing harder.

By the time Coach finally blows the whistle for the last time, signaling the end of practice, I'm drenched in sweat, my shirt clinging to my back, my muscles screaming in protest. I collapse onto the grass, rolling onto my back as the too-bright sun blazes overhead. The sky is a piercing blue, but it might as well be black for how drained I feel.

Julio walks by and taps my leg with his foot. "You alive?"

"Barely," I mutter, my voice hoarse from exertion, my chest heaving as I try to catch my breath. The scent of earth and sweat fills my nose, grounding me even as my body protests every movement. "I'm hitting the showers, then I'm crashing. Need a few hours of sleep before I can function again."

"Same, bro." He reaches down, pulling me to my feet. My legs wobble beneath me, muscles protesting the shift in weight. "Good work out there, though. We've still got a shot this season."

I nod, exhaustion weighing me down, but beneath it, there's a sense of satisfaction. Despite the pain, despite the gaps in our team, there's something here—a thread of hope, a shot at redemption. We may be down a few good players, but we're not out yet. Not by a long shot.

eleven

CECILIA

THE SECOND I STEP INSIDE, the cool air wraps around me like a safety net, easing the tension in my shoulders. Relief floods through me as I breathe in the familiar scent of home—freshly brewed espresso and the lingering aroma of garlic and basil from whatever Mom's been cooking today. It grounds me in a way only home can. Well, home and Gabriel, I suppose.

My parents greet me as I enter, smiles on their faces, completely unaware of the chaos that unraveled last night. No signs of panic, no sharp questions—just the soft murmur of their usual small talk.

I had texted Dad from Gabriel's, letting him know I'd be staying the night. But still, a part of me expected my mom to bombard me with questions the second I walked through the door. She's always so nosy, especially when it comes to Gabriel.

"Did you have a good time last night?" Mom asks, her voice light and casual as if nothing's wrong. She glances at my dad, who's already buried in his newspaper, one hand lazily stirring a cup of coffee. The clink of his spoon against the ceramic mug blends with the familiar scent of Italian food filling the air.

I force a smile, the muscles in my face feeling tight. "Yeah, it was nice," I say, keeping my tone as easy as theirs. Relief loosens the knot in my stomach. I don't linger—just a couple of nods and polite chuckles before I make my escape upstairs. Each step feels lighter, the distance between me and their questions a necessary buffer.

Shutting the door behind me, I let out a sigh of relief. Thank God. They didn't know. They didn't have to worry.

I flop down onto my bed, the mattress sinking beneath me like it's trying to swallow my exhaustion whole. My phone catches my eye—its screen cracked from last night, a reminder of everything I want to forget. Great. Just what I need, another thing to deal with. Swiping through the notifications, I quickly clear the missed calls from Gabriel and the rest of the guys. But my attention sticks to the missed calls and texts from Adriana.

I hit call before I can second-guess myself, the trill of the outgoing ring pulsing in my ear, my heart matching its rhythm. After the second ring, she answers, bombarding me with a flood of questions—no buffer, no warning.

"Are you okay? Julio called last night and said you were missing, but he wouldn't give me any details," she huffs. "He said you and Gabe got into a fight, and you weren't answering your phone, but seriously, where the hell have you been? I get ignoring the guys—if Gabriel was being an asshole, I'd ignore him too," she grumbles, her tone softening as she adds, "But you didn't answer me either. What gives? And don't lie. Are you okay?"

I consider making something up or blowing off the question, but lying to Adriana doesn't sit right with me. Besides, I'm tired of carrying this by myself.

"Well ..." My chest tightens, hesitation curling in my gut. I can just tell her. She won't be mad like Gabriel. At least, I don't think she will. I doubt she'll be happy but—*Screw it.* I need to tell someone, and Adriana is the safest option I have. She's the least likely to judge me for it and the most likely to understand.

I take a breath and dive in, giving her the quick version of last night's events. "Gabriel and I went to his mom's wedding, and ... well, she definitely wasn't thrilled to see him."

Adriana's response is immediate, but her tone remains steady. "That sucks," she says, her voice even, controlled. I know she's absorbing it, processing it in her own quiet way. She and Gabe used to be close, so she's already familiar with the messy dynamic between him and his parents.

"Yeah, it wasn't great. I could see how much it hurt him, and I tried talking to him, but he was just ... pissed. Really pissed. He lashed out, blamed me for the whole thing going sideways." I pause, feeling the sting of those words again.

"Of course he did," Adriana says, her voice so matter-of-fact it almost stings. "Like you could've known his mom was gonna act like that."

"I know, right?" I huff, rubbing my temples. "But he was hurt, so he lashed out at me. You know how it goes. Hurt people, hurt people."

Adriana lets out a soft exhale, not quite a sigh. "Yeah, I get it." There's a beat of silence before she adds, "You're a lot more forgiving than I'd be. I wouldn't have let him off that easy."

I try to laugh, but it comes out weak. "It's fine now. He apologized. I get why he was upset, and I don't hold it against him." I hesitate, knowing the next part is going to hit harder. "But that's not even the worst of it."

Adriana's voice stays neutral, like she's waiting. "There's more?"

I nod, even though she can't see me. "After he stormed off, he sent me home with Felix. I was upset, too, so when I got home, I went for a walk to clear my head." I hesitate again, chewing on my bottom lip. "That's when things really went south."

"South how?" Her tone remains calm, but I can sense the subtle shift—she's on alert now, piecing things together.

I take a deep breath. "Austin's mom found me. Cornered me while I was alone."

Adriana doesn't react at first, just a pause that stretches longer than I expect. "What do you mean, she *found* you?"

"I was going for a walk. She pulled up with her driver and sorta cornered me on the side of the road. I tried to walk away, but they made it pretty clear I didn't have a choice." I swallow hard. "So, I got in the car."

Another pause. Then, Adriana says quietly, "You got in the car with her." It's not a question. More like she's repeating the words to herself, trying to make sense of them.

"I didn't have a choice," I explain, the defensiveness creeping into my voice despite myself. "Trust me, I didn't *want* to. But she wasn't giving me any other option."

Adriana's response is slow, deliberate. "Okay. So what did she want?"

"She was freaking out because Austin made bail, and they couldn't find him. She wanted to make sure he wouldn't come after me. Not because she gives a shit about me, obviously. But so Austin doesn't land himself in more hot water. So, she kept me with her until her husband tracked him down."

A low exhale escapes Adriana. "She kept you with her," she repeats, her voice steady, though I can hear the tension beneath it. "And you're okay?"

"Yeah," I say quickly, needing to reassure her. "I'm fine. She didn't hurt me. But she talked about this plea deal. Five years for Austin, three for Gregory and Parker. Court-ordered therapy for all of them when they get out."

Adriana is quiet for a moment. When she finally speaks, her voice is calm, but I sense the shift in her energy. "And you're considering it."

It's not a question. She's always been good at reading between the lines, even when she's holding back her own reactions.

"I don't know," I admit. "There's no guarantee Austin will get more than five years if we go to trial, and Gregory and Parker? They'll walk. I'm just ... I'm not sure I have the energy to go through a long trial, and honestly, I'm scared of the outcome of one."

Her silence lingers again, but I know she's turning it over in her mind, weighing my words.

"You've clearly thought about this," she says after a beat, her tone careful. "Which means you've already gone through all of your options. What's holding you back?"

I bite my lip, my chest tightening. "I guess ... I just need someone to tell me I'm not crazy for considering it."

"You're not crazy," she says. "You're doing what you need to do to protect yourself. That's not crazy."

Relief washes over me, but it's tinged with guilt. "Gabe doesn't know yet," I confess, my voice quieter.

Adriana doesn't react, at least not outwardly. But I know she's filing the information away like she always does, her mind working through the implications. "That's a mistake," she says. "You need to tell him. Sooner rather than later. Accepting a plea deal is no small thing."

"I know," I murmur, feeling the weight of it settle back on my shoulders. "I will. Just ... not today."

"Not today," she echoes, her voice level, but there's a firm undertone. "But soon. Promise me."

"Yeah. Soon."

Adriana has always been like this—never one to push too hard, never making things more complicated than they need to be. It's a kind of stability I've come to rely on, even when her own emotions stay beneath the surface.

"You wanna grab coffee this week?" she asks after a beat, the shift in tone subtle but noticeable.

I manage a small smile. "Yeah, I'd like that."

"Cool. Text me when you're free."

After we hang up, I grab my laptop and start chipping away at schoolwork, but my mind is elsewhere. The conversation with Adriana lingers in my head, as does the conversation I know I need to have with Gabriel.

Seriously, when is all of the drama in my life going to end?

My phone chirps and a text from Gabriel illuminates my screen, pulling me out of my thoughts.

> Gabriel: I'm picking you up in 30. Dress comfortably.

A thrill of excitement shoots through me—followed by a twinge of guilt. It's only been a couple of hours since I saw him this morning, but I already miss him. Still, the conversation I'm avoiding weighs heavy in the back of my mind. Whatever he's planning, might as well enjoy it before dropping the bomb that's bound to ruin everything.

Closing my laptop, I scramble to my feet and rush to the bathroom.

After the world's fastest shower in the history of showers, I towel off my hair, finger-combing it into a messy braid. I throw on ripped jeans and an oversized t-shirt, slipping into my checkered Vans before pausing at my dresser. My fingers hover over my stack of bracelets, the ones I usually wear to cover my scars. But today ... I don't feel the need to hide them.

The doorbell rings, and I rush downstairs, tugging the door open to find Gabriel standing there, looking effortlessly sexy in low-slung jeans and a fitted white t-shirt. My eyes can't help but sweep over his broad shoulders, the way the fabric pulls tight across his chest.

No sexy thoughts, Cecilia. We're taking things slow, not daydreaming about how to jump his bones.

"Hey," I say, grinning despite my nerves.

His smile is just as big. "You ready?"

Before I can answer, the sound of a car door slamming pulls our attention. I turn just in time to see my attorney, Mr. Ayala, stepping out of his sedan, his expression grim. My stomach tightens. This can't be good.

Gabriel's brow furrows. "Were you expecting him today?"

"No." My voice comes out more uncertain than I'd like.

I step aside, and Gabriel follows me into the house, his expression leery at the unexpected guest. The air feels suddenly too thick, the easy mood Gabriel and I had just moments ago shattered.

"Ms. Russo, Mr. Herrera," Mr. Ayala greets us. "Do you have a moment?" The question is directed at me, but it feels like a dismissal for Gabriel.

"We were actually about to head out," Gabriel interjects, his tone casual, but I don't miss the edge to it. "But we've got a few minutes. Right?" He glances at me, his smile tight, as if asking for permission to stay.

"Yeah." I manage. Whatever this is, I'm not ready. "What's up?"

Mr. Ayala doesn't seem happy about having an audience, which should've been my first warning.

"I'll get straight to the point," Mr. Ayala begins, his voice clipped. "I spoke with Mr. Holt's counsel this morning, and there's been talk of a plea agreement."

My stomach drops. Already? Jaymin didn't waste any time.

Gabriel shakes his head in disbelief. "No way," he snaps, his voice rising. "Tell them to shove their deal where the sun doesn't shine. Cecilia's not about to accept whatever bullshit offer they're making."

"Actually ..." Shit. I was not prepared for this.

Gabriel's head snaps toward me, his golden brown eyes darkening. "Did you already know about this?"

I shift on my feet, my pulse quickening, avoiding his gaze. I do not want to have this conversation right now. "I ... Umm. Sort of. I spoke with Jaymin Holt last night and she offered five years for Austin, three for Gregory and Parker—"

"Fucking hell!" Gabriel's voice explodes, his hand flying to his hair in frustration. "You talked to her? That's where you were?" His eyes bore into mine, and I flinch.

My pulse quickens. His anger is a palpable force, like a heat wave pressing down on me. "It's not what you think—"

"You can't seriously be considering this!" His hands rake through his hair, his eyes blazing. "He's facing fifteen years to life, Cecilia. You're honestly considering letting that asshole get off with five? You can't trust anything that comes out of that family's mouth. You know that. I can't believe you'd—"

"Gabe—"

"After everything he did? Why would you even agree to speak with them?" His voice is raw and dripping with disappointment.

I flinch again. I didn't expect him to take it well, but the intensity of his disapproval ... it cuts deeper than I thought.

"I'm not doing this for him." My voice cracks under the weight of my frustration. "I'm doing it for me."

Gabriel's jaw tightens, his chest rising and falling as he tries to rein in his temper. His eyes search mine, disbelief flickering there. "For you?" he mutters, low and dangerous. "How is this for you?"

I step forward, hands clenched at my sides. "If we go to trial, there's no guarantee Holt gets more than five years. And Gregory and Parker? They walk without this deal. I can't live with that, Gabriel. I won't. Not if there's another way." My voice strengthens, resolve unfurling in my chest.

Gabriel mutters a curse under his breath, his body tense. "You should have talked to me. You know how worried I was last night. We all were."

"I know," I whisper, my throat tight. "And I was going to. But you stormed off, remember? I couldn't exactly call you when she showed up, and even if I could've, you wouldn't have answered."

Silence stretches between us, the weight of my words sinking in. Gabriel's eyes lock on mine. It was a low blow, and part of me regrets it, but it's still the truth.

"Tell him," I say, turning to Mr. Ayala. "Explain what happens if we go to trial."

Mr. Ayala clears his throat. "A trial like this is going to be long and arduous, with no guarantee when it comes to sentencing. Without this deal, it's likely that the other boys walk free. The charges are too light and for both boys, it's only their first offense. Neither has a record and both come from well-known families. The prosecutor will opt to focus their efforts on Mr. Holt and wash their hands clean of the others. This arrangement ensures all three perpetrators face jail time."

Gabriel's nostrils flare, his hands now fisted at his sides. "But five years? It isn't enough. Holt will get out, and then what?"

I swallow hard, my voice barely audible. "I'll be free of him. I'll have finished college. I can move. Start over."

Gabriel turns away, glaring out the window, his frustration simmering in the air between us.

"If we go to trial," Mr Ayala says, "there is always the risk of Austin Holt walking free. I'm very good at my job," he assures us, "but you should both understand that being found 'not guilty,' is always a possibility in situations like this."

Which is exactly the reason I'm giving thought to Jaymin's offer at all.

"I should've told you sooner," I admit, my voice shaky. I don't want to fight with him, but this is still my decision. "But this is my choice. My life."

Gabriel finally looks back at me, his eyes a mix of anger and hurt. "We're supposed to be in this together, Cecilia. You said you wanted a real relationship, but this—" He shakes his head. "You can't shut me out of the big decisions like this."

Tears prick my eyes, but I blink them back, standing my ground. "I can when they're my decisions to make." My voice thickens, but I push through. "I know you don't want to hear that, and I'm sorry. I really was going to tell you. But I need you to understand that I'm doing what I need to do to move on. I want us to be a team. To be on the same page. But I also need you to support me, even when I'm making decisions you don't necessarily agree with."

Gabriel's shoulders sag, some of the fight leaving him. "Right," he mutters. "Looks like you've already made up your mind."

"I'm sorry," I whisper. "I think I have."

He steps forward, pulling me into his arms, and I bury my face in his chest, breathing him in.

"I just need this to be over," I murmur, my voice barely holding steady.

Gabriel presses his lips to the top of my head. His touch is gentler now, but there's still tension coiled in his body. "I know, baby. I'm trying to understand that. But I also need you to understand that if we're going to make this work, you have to start letting me in."

I close my eyes, trying to block out the mess of emotions swirling inside me. "I'll try."

twelve

GABRIEL

I'M HOLDING on by a thread, frustration simmering just beneath the surface, as the reality of the situation slips further out of my control.

Mr. Ayala leaves, promising to schedule an appointment with Cecilia and her father soon so they can discuss the particulars of the plea agreement should she decide to move forward, and fuck, it seems like she does.

I bite my tongue and brace myself for her words as Cecilia shows him the door. She waves him goodbye, closes the door, and slumps against it.

"Not really the way I saw today going," she mutters.

Taking a deep breath, I set my frustration aside and remind myself why I'm here. We were going out. I had everything planned. No way in hell am I going to let this new revelation throw a wrench in my plans.

We're going to have ups and downs. Disagreements. But part of being in a relationship is working through disagreements like this. I take another deep breath. I just gotta be calm and collected so we can talk through this.

"Why did you decide to meet with Holt's mom?" I ask, keeping my tone even.

Cecilia chews on her bottom lip. "I didn't exactly decide to meet with her ... it err ... it wasn't really planned," she says.

"What is that supposed to mean?" My voice tightens despite my best efforts.

She rubs the back of her neck and glances at me. "Can we just ... go out? If we start talking about this now, you're going to get mad, and I really want us to have a good day."

I pause, exhaling through my nose. "I'm not going to get mad." The way she looks at me says otherwise, and it stings, but I push it down. "I swear. I just ... need to understand. Keeping me in the dark like this, it's messing with my head. Help a guy out because I'm low-key spiraling here, babe."

Her shoulders relax a little, her expression softening. "You promise?"

"I promise." I sigh. "Just talk to me."

"And you'll let me finish my story. No interruptions and no freaking out."

I nod.

"Okay." She takes my hand and pulls me upstairs, like she needs the comfort of familiar spaces to say everything she needs to. She sits on the bed, her back against the headboard, tapping the space beside her. I join her, wrapping my arm around her as she leans into me, and I steel myself for whatever's coming.

"After Felix dropped me off, I went for a walk and—"

She spends the next ten minutes telling me what happened, and true to my word, I don't interrupt her. Not once. Where I fuck up, however, is that I am absolutely freaking the fuck out and it is taking every ounce of my control to keep that to shit inside my own head because What. The. Fuck?

When she finishes, I can barely breathe.

"So, that's sorta everything," she says quietly, almost like she's waiting for me to blow up.

I nod, even though my chest is tight with emotions I can't fully unravel. "Mmhmm." I don't trust myself to speak right now. I'm doing everything I can to rein my temper in. And it's not like I'm pissed with Cecilia. She's the victim in all this. But fuck if I can help it, because despite knowing that, I'm seeing fucking red.

"What are you thinking?" she asks softly, shifting against me.

I pull her closer, pressing a kiss to the top of her head to keep myself calm. "I'm not really thinking about anything," I lie. Truth is, I'm thinking about a million things, and none of them feel good.

She glances up at me, searching my face, trying to read what's going on inside my head. "Are you sure? Because you feel ... tense."

I force out a laugh but it's strained. "Yeah, just ... processing." *Trying not to lose my shit,* I don't add.

Her fingers trace lazy patterns on my arm, and it's comforting in a way that makes the frustration even harder to deal with. I want to protect her, to make all this shit go away, but I can't. Not when she's considering letting the guy who ruined her life walk away with just a few years behind bars.

"And you're not mad?"

I shake my head.

I wish I could give her more than that right now, but I'm still working through the fact that she was fucking *kidnapped* by Holt's psychotic mother and that she's even entertaining the idea of a plea deal. *Five years?* It's a slap on the wrist for what that asshole did to her.

"How do you feel about the deal?" I ask, my voice tight.

At the end of it all, that's really what matters. I want what's best for Cecilia, and I don't want her manipulated into agreeing to something she doesn't want. But if this is what she wants ... what she *really* wants ... then who am I to object?

She shrugs, eyes dropping to the space between us. "I don't know ... It feels like it's the only way to make sure Gregory and Parker don't get away scot-free. I ... I don't think I'm okay with that."

In her shoes, I know I wouldn't be. It's just ... fuck. There is no clear-cut path here.

"What if he gets out early? What if he's back before you're ready?"

"I'll never be ready," she admits, her voice barely above a whisper. "But at least this way, I'll have time to make a plan. I can finish school, get away from Richland if I want to. I'll have time to rebuild my life without having to look over my shoulder."

Her words gut me. I hate that she feels like she has to make this choice. I hate that I can't do anything but watch as she tries to piece herself back together. But I can't argue with her logic. She's trying to find peace in a situation that offers none.

I stay quiet for a beat, just holding her, letting her presence ground me. I promised her I wouldn't freak out. So I won't. For her sake, I'll keep it together.

"I hate that you're going through this," I finally say, my voice rough. "I hate that I couldn't protect you from any of it. And I'm trying to understand, I really am ... but part of me wishes you wouldn't consider a deal. Part of me wants to ask you to push forward. To see the trial through and let the chips fall where they may, but," I take a deep breath. "You have to do what's best for you, and no matter what, I'll be here to support you."

"Thank you," she whispers, her fingers tightening around mine. "I know you want to protect me, and I love that about you, but ... I think this is what I need to move on."

Love? Did she mean to say that? Does saying she loves *that* about me mean she loves *me?* Like she's in love with me or maybe falling in love with me?

No.

I'm getting ahead of myself here, but fuck. I like the sound of that.

I pull back just enough to see her face, but she's avoiding my gaze now, her cheeks flushed with embarrassment. I don't ask her to explain herself or to repeat what she said, even though my heart is hammering in my chest at the thought of hearing those words from her again. Instead, I kiss the top of her head, letting the moment settle.

"Okay," I say softly. "If this is what you need ... then I'll support your decisions. But you have to promise me something."

She looks up at me, her brows drawn in confusion. "What?"

"You have to let me in from now on. No more hiding things, no more making decisions like this on your own. We're in this together, Cecilia. You don't have to carry it all by yourself. I know we agreed to slow, but slow doesn't mean solo. Alright?"

Her eyes soften, and she nods slowly. "Okay."

"Good." I tighten my arms around her, pressing my cheek to her hair. "Because I'm not going anywhere, no matter what happens. You and me? We're a team now. Got it?"

She blinks up at me, a soft smile tugging at her lips. "Okay."

I know this isn't over and I know I should probably call the police. Report Austin's mom for abduction or something, but I'll let Mr. Ayala figure out how he wants to handle that mess.

After a few minutes, Cecilia shifts in my arms, looking up at me with a teasing smile. "So ... weren't we supposed to go somewhere? Or did I manage to derail all your plans?"

I chuckle, the tension finally easing from my shoulders. "Nice try, but you didn't derail shit. We've got a date to head out to."

Her eyes brighten, and I can't help but smile. *That's my girl.*

"Where are we going?" she asks, slipping off the bed.

"It's a surprise."

thirteen
CECILIA

THE PIER FEELS like something out of a dream—or maybe a nightmare. It's deserted, broken down, with boarded-up shops and the faded colors of a place that once thrived but now barely clings to life. The creak of the wooden boards beneath our feet is the only sound besides the distant crash of waves. Salt hangs in the air, thick and heavy, like it's trying to settle in my lungs. I take a deep breath, feeling it sink into me. Somehow, it calms me.

"This place is incredible," I whisper, more to myself than to Gabriel. He's a few steps ahead, leading the way toward the rundown mini golf course at the far end of the pier. The wind catches in his dark hair, tousling it, making him look almost boyish.

He stops and turns, a small smile playing on his lips. "Used to be," he says, his voice low. "Back when I was a kid, this place was always packed. People everywhere. Ice cream stands, the smell of churros in the air. The arcade would be lit up, and you'd hear the clink of quarters dropping into machines. Now

..." He gestures around us to the broken pieces of what once was. "Now it's just this."

I follow him past what's left of the arcade, the windows dark and smudged with years of neglect. But there's something about it. I can see what it must've been like—laughter and life. And I understand why he comes here. It's not about the place as it is now. It's about what it used to be and the feeling it evokes.

"It's kind of perfect," I say. "Quiet. Empty. Peaceful."

His eyes meet mine, and for a moment, something flickers between us—understanding, maybe. I'm not sure. But then he nods and keeps walking.

We reach the mini golf course, and it's ridiculous in the best possible way. Plastic animals faded by the sun, a couple of torn-up windmills, and rusted metal obstacles that look like they'd fall apart if we touched them too hard. But it's charming in a strange, forgotten way.

"Are we breaking in?" I ask, half-smiling.

Gabriel smirks. "It's not breaking in if no one cares anymore."

With a quick glance around, he lifts a section of the flimsy fence, and we slip inside. There's something thrilling about it, something that makes my heart beat a little faster. I haven't done anything like this—anything remotely reckless—in so long. Maybe ever.

He grabs an old, chipped club, tossing me one as well. "You play?"

"I'm terrible at it," I admit as I take the club. "But I'll still beat you."

He laughs, the sound rich and warm, echoing off the empty pier. "We'll see."

We start playing, moving from hole to hole, and I'm terrible, just like I said I'd be. Gabriel lets me win, I can tell, but I don't call him out on it. I just enjoy the ease of it, the simplicity. For once, it's not about saving me or dragging me through the mess I've been stuck in. It's just this. The two of us, playing this stupid game in a forgotten place filled with forgotten memories.

As we play, we swap stories, trading pieces of our pasts like puzzle pieces. I tell him about my summers as a kid, about the trips to Yosemite my parents and I used to take before Dad got into politics and got too busy for extended vacations.

He listens, really listens, and when it's his turn, he talks about his childhood—about Carlos.

"We were twins," he says, lining up a shot at the next hole. "But we couldn't have been more different. Carlos was ... impulsive. Always getting into trouble, always dragging me along with him." He pauses, the ball rolling lazily down the green. "Fought like cats and dogs most days. But still, he was ... you know, my other half. He was my brother."

He doesn't look at me, his gaze fixed on the horizon. I don't push, just wait.

"He got in with the wrong crowd in high school," Gabriel continues, his voice tightening. "Started drinking, using. I think —no, I know—he was self-medicating. Depression, not that he'd ever admit it out loud. He didn't talk about it, but the signs were all there if I'd bothered to pay attention."

Gabriel shrugs. "We started growing apart sophomore year of high school but I didn't really think anything of it. I was focused on soccer back then and sports weren't really Carlos's thing. When he got into drugs, he turned into a different person. He was volatile. Always picking fights and causing trouble. Between the drugs and the parties, it was obvious he was spiraling. I figured I'd give him his space and sooner or later, he'd hit rock bottom. And I told myself when he did, I'd be there to help him up. He was my brother. I had his back. Always. But he was too far gone by the time I realized just how bad shit really was with him. That he was in too deep to find his way to the surface."

His words hang in the air, heavy like the salt on my skin. The ocean waves crash behind us, and for a second, it feels like the world narrows down to this moment, to Gabriel standing there, raw and open.

"I'm sorry," I say, the words are inadequate but they're all I have.

He nods, and when he finally looks at me, his eyes are darker, more vulnerable than I've ever seen. "It's why I was so pushy with you in the beginning," he says. "Did I ever tell you I was the one who found him?"

I shake my head.

"He came home high one night and my mom flipped out on him. I remember her screaming at him, telling him what a disappointment he was and that the very sight of him made her sick."

Moisture pricks the backs of my eyes.

"I should have said something. Maybe if I did he ..." He shakes his head. "It doesn't matter. That night, Carlos locked himself in his room. We had one of those Jack and Jill bathrooms between our bedrooms, and I remember hearing the water turn on. I figured he was maybe taking a cold shower. Trying to sober up. But the water was on for a really long time. I got this feeling in my chest." He presses his hand over his heart. "It was tight and the pain was unlike anything I'd experienced before. I knew something was wrong but I didn't know what. I knocked on the door, but he never answered. I pounded on the damn thing. I knew he was pissed off, and ignoring me was common behavior for him, but I don't know, I just couldn't shake the feeling. My mom and dad had gone out that night after the fight so it was just the two of us and I started to get worried."

I swallow hard, the weight of what he's saying sinking in. He's been carrying this—his brother, his guilt—like a chain around his neck.

"I broke through the door and nearly dislocated my shoulder in the process," he says. "And then there he was," his voice grows thick. "I knew as soon as I saw him that it was too late. He was already gone. There were pills spilled out over the counter. An empty bottle of Hornitos beside the tub. And there was blood." A muscle ticks in his jaw. "There was so much fucking blood."

Without hesitation, I go to him and wrap my arms around Gabriel's waist. "I'm so sorry you had to see that," I tell him, and it's then I realize what finding me must have done to him. No wonder he was angry. I can't imagine the sort of emotions that must have triggered in him. "And I'm sorry you were the one to find me. You never should have had to—"

"No," he says, pulling me impossibly closer to his chest. "I'm sorry you found yourself in a position where you felt that was your only option. But I'm not sorry I'm the one who found you. As fucked up as that day was, it led me to you. No way would I change that."

I take a deep breath, letting the salt air fill my lungs, and I tilt my head back to meet his gaze. "You don't have to keep trying to save me," I tell him.

His jaw clenches, and for a second, I think he'll argue. But then he just nods. "I think I understand that now. But I'm not going anywhere. I want to wade through the muck with you. I won't leave you on your own and hope you find your way out on the other side."

The sound of the ocean fills the silence between us, and despite the heaviness of the conversation, I feel ... lighter.

Gabriel squeezes me once, then pulls back, a small smile on his lips. "Come on. I think we've got a few more holes left."

fourteen

CECILIA

LESS THAN A WEEK goes by before being home 24/7 starts to get to me. Suffocates me, really. Maybe that's a little dramatic. Probably not, but after everything with Austin, I don't know. I guess I thought finishing the semester online was the right move. It would give me some space to breathe. To forget about all the awful things that happened to me. But instead of peace, it feels like I've traded one set of problems for another. I thought stepping away from campus, away from the chaos, would help.

But I think I made a mistake. A colossal one.

The noise in my head isn't gone, it's louder in the silence of this house.

Mom is a stay-at-home wife, and while she has charity functions and the mayor's office stuff to keep her busy, lately it feels like I've suddenly become her full-time project. She's always hovering, checking in, bringing me food like I'm going to waste away if she doesn't. I get it—she's worried. But I'm not a child. I know she means well, but she doesn't exactly pick the right moments. Like in the middle of my online lectures, when she insists on staying for a chat.

I've given her my class schedule, but it doesn't matter. I'm a body in the house. A warm body means company. Since most of my coursework is self-directed, she's taken that as an open invitation to drag me along on errands or expect me to keep her company all day.

Wednesday, she drags me to gentle yoga at the women's club. Thursday, it's brunch with the ladies from Dad's office. By Friday? I'm seconds from screaming into a pillow.

So I do. Quietly. Right before I leave to meet Adriana for coffee before Mom has a chance to add anything to my schedule.

Parking my Jeep, I head into The Howling Cup and find her already waiting for me at one of the corner tables.

"Hey," I call out. "Did you already order?"

She lifts her mug in the air, and I stick my tongue out at her before dropping my bag on the empty seat across from her. "Rude. Give me two minutes to grab my own and I'll be right back."

"Take your time," she says. Her tone is light, but her fingers are tapping lightly against her cup—like she's keeping track of the seconds I'm gone.

I shrug it off and head to the counter to order my coffee.

I order their special—a white chocolate, huckleberry mocha made with white coffee. It's surprisingly good and it definitely hits the spot. Making my way back to our table, I take my seat and eye Adriana curiously.

"Who are you looking at?" I ask.

Adriana's eyes don't move from the table across the room, and I follow her line of sight, curious. She's staring at a group of guys, all seated together with an easy, laid-back vibe, their laughter carrying across the café. There's a pile of hockey sticks resting against the wall next to them, the oversized gear bags thrown haphazardly around their feet making it pretty clear these guys are on the university hockey team.

But it's one guy in particular who seems to have captured Adriana's attention. He's tall, with messy black hair that falls over his forehead, and even from where I'm sitting, I can see the sharp angle of his jaw. He's got this flirty smile on his face, and the way he keeps glancing over at Adriana ... it's like he's just waiting for her to notice him back.

"Adriana," I tease, nudging her foot under the table. "You're practically drooling. Who's the guy?"

She blinks, tearing her gaze away from him to look at me. There's a brief flicker of annoyance—like I've pulled her from something she didn't want to leave—but it's gone as quickly as it came. Her smile is instant, but something in her eyes shifts, like she's forcing herself to focus on me when just seconds ago, she was a million miles away. "I am not drooling," she protests, though her voice wavers. I arch a brow, calling bullshit.

"I see the way he's looking at you. Come on, spill."

Adriana glances over at him again, biting her lip before finally sighing. Her hands fidget with her mug, spinning it in slow circles as if she's trying to work out exactly what to say. Or maybe how much to say. "His name's Kenji. He asked me out the other day."

My eyes widen, excitement bubbling up inside me. "What?

Why the hell didn't you lead with that? When are you guys going out?"

She takes a slow sip of her coffee, dragging it out way longer than necessary. "I don't know. I told him I'd think about it."

"Think about it? Girl, he's hot! You should definitely say yes."

Adriana shrugs, but I can tell by the way her fingers tap nervously on the table that she's not completely against the idea. She shrugs again, and her shoulders tense, like she's waiting for me to push. She's looking down now, her eyes a little wide, almost like she's scared to make a decision. "I don't know. He seems nice, but ... you know how it is. He's a hockey player. And you know the reputation they have."

There's a flash of something in her eyes—doubt, maybe? Fear? —but it's gone as quickly as it appeared.

She's talking, but it feels rehearsed—like she's listing reasons to convince herself, not me.

I roll my eyes. "Not all athletes are players, Adriana. Look at Gabriel—he's different."

She gives me a pointed look. "Yeah, but Gabriel wasn't always like that. You are the only girl he's ever been like this with. What if Kenji's just hoping for an easy lay? I ... I'm not great at judging people's intentions." Her voice drops lower, quieter now, as if she's revealing more than she meant to. Her fingers tighten around her mug.

"Or," I counter, leaning forward, "what if he's a good guy who actually likes you? Sometimes you just have to put yourself out there. Besides, he's cute."

Adriana glances back at him, and I don't miss the small smile

130

playing on her lips. "He is cute," she admits, her cheeks flushing. "But I don't know— "

I shake my head. "It's just one date, right? You're not committing to anything serious."

She hesitates, her gaze drifting back to Kenji, who's now laughing with his friends but sneaking glances in her direction when he thinks she's not looking. It's obvious—he's waiting for her to say something. To make a move or approach his table maybe.

"You know what?" I say, giving her a nudge. "What if we do a double date? You guys with Gabriel and I?"

Adriana freezes, her fingers tightening around her cup. There's a flicker of something behind her eyes—hesitation, or maybe even doubt—like she's unsure whether to trust me with this decision. Then she releases a breath, her shoulders loosening like she's letting herself settle into the idea. "Okay. Fine. I'll go out with him, but you're coming too."

Victory. "Deal," I say, grinning. "Now, text him and set it up before you chicken out."

She laughs, pulling out her phone. "You're relentless, you know that?"

"Of course, I am. Someone's gotta make sure you don't let a good thing slip away."

Adriana pulls out her phone, her fingers moving fast over the screen like she's trying to get it over with before she changes her mind. She hesitates for a second, her lips pressing together tightly before she places the phone face down on the table, almost like it's a challenge. "Okay, it's done. Happy now?"

"Ecstatic." I give her a wink, and she rolls her eyes, but her smile is softer now, a little less forced.

We sit in comfortable silence for a moment, sipping our drinks, and I can't help but feel a little proud of myself. Kenji's clearly interested, and Adriana deserves to have some fun. Plus, it's nice to focus on someone else's love life for a change.

Her phone buzzes on the table, and she glances at it before looking up at me, eyes wide. "He's good with the double date idea. He wants to know if Tuesday next week sounds good?"

I lean back in my chair, a smug smile on my face. "It's a date!"

Adriana shakes her head. "You're the worst."

"Or the best," I counter, grinning. "This will be fun. Trust me."

"MmmHmm. Might want to let your boyfriend know what you signed him up for."

Adriana's words land softly, but they carry an edge, like she's testing them out—trying to figure out how I'll react. Boyfriend. It's not like I haven't thought about it—Gabriel being my boyfriend—but hearing someone else say it out loud makes it feel more real. Like we've crossed some invisible line from casual to something more. And damn if that doesn't give me all the warm fuzzies.

I bite my lip, trying to suppress the goofy grin spreading across my face, but Adriana catches it. "Oh my God, you're totally swooning."

"No, I'm not," I say, even though we both know I am.

She arches a brow. "Liar."

I swallow the immediate defensiveness that rises, brushing it off with a laugh. Okay, fine. I totally am. But I mean, can you blame me? Gabriel Herrera is just so ... *great*. And hearing him referred to as my *boyfriend*? It feels good. Better than good. Like maybe this whole "taking things slow" thing is exactly what we need.

I let out a little sigh. "Okay, fine. Maybe I am swooning a little. It's just ... I don't know. It feels nice. Normal, even."

Adriana smirks. "Normal isn't a word I'd use to describe you two, but I get it. He's good for you, Cecilia. Even I have to admit that."

I smile into my cup, taking a sip of my coffee. "Yeah, he is." And even though we've been through a lot—more than most people our age should have to deal with—I like where we're headed. It's not perfect, but it feels solid. Real.

Adriana's phone buzzes again, pulling her attention back to the screen. "Alright. Tuesday is a go. You are not allowed to bail on me," she says, holding up her phone. "Now all you need to do is tell Gabriel and remember, no bailing!"

I roll my eyes, but the smile on my face betrays me. "He'll be fine with it."

"You say that like you know he won't complain about being forced on a double date without his consent. I assure you, he will. Gabriel doesn't mingle outside of his crew. He won't like it."

I laugh. "He's not going to complain. He'll probably just grumble a little and then go along with it because that's what he does."

She gives me a look. "For you. Gabriel only ever bends for you."

I shrug, but inside I'm doing mental backflips. "Maybe."

Adriana leans back in her chair, a satisfied smirk on her face. "It will be nice to go out, I suppose. Kenji seems like a decent guy. I don't get the typical asshole jock vibe from him that seems to follow most PacNorth athletes around."

"Hey!" I admonish.

"The guys obviously excluded."

"That's better," I tell her.

And if he's not," she shrugs, "one date won't kill me."

"Way to be positive."

Adriana grins, nudging my foot under the table. "Yup. I'm just a regular old ball of sunshine."

fifteen

GABRIEL

I'M STRETCHED out on the couch, my phone in one hand, half-listening to Julio and Deacon argue about some soccer game they're rewatching. The faint hum of the TV mixes with their voices, a background noise I've gotten too used to. Felix is at his parents' visiting his sister. Atticus had some study group thing, so it's just the three of us.

Should be a pretty chill night. But I'm restless.

Scratch that—I'm agitated.

I haven't had a minute alone with Cecilia all week, and it's driving me out of my damn mind. Every time we get together, we've got an audience. My roommates are home, or it's her parents, hovering like she's going to break at any second.

I need to figure out a way to maneuver some alone time with my girl.

My phone buzzes, yanking me out of my thoughts.

A double date? I swipe my thumb over the screen, reading the message twice. I was hoping for some one-on-one time. Just us. Instead, I get to share her. Again. This time with Adriana and whoever's dumb enough to think he can keep up with her.

I drag a hand over my face, the slightest chuckle slipping out before I can stop it.

"What's up?" Julio asks, his voice cutting through Deacon's ongoing commentary on the screen. He's leaning back, arms crossed, the black ink of the rosary on his right hand standing out against his tan skin. I've always found it ironic—he's got that cross and beads tattooed, but I've never seen him step foot inside a church.

"Just got a text from Cecilia," I mutter, tossing my phone onto the coffee table. It clatters against the wood, and the sound pulls Julio's eyes away from the screen for the first time since they put the game on. "She's setting up a double date with Adriana and some guy."

Julio's posture shifts, subtle but telling. His shoulders stiffen, his jaw ticking like he's just bit into something sour.

"Adriana's going on a date?"

I glance at him, raising an eyebrow. "Yeah. Tuesday."

"Who's it with?" he asks, trying for casual, but his tone? It's anything but. The edge in his voice is sharp, and the way he grips the couch cushion has me intrigued.

138

"I don't know." I sit up a little straighter, smirking. "You jealous or something?"

Julio shrugs, but his eyes flick toward my phone like he's thinking about snatching it from the table. "No. Just ... curious."

Curious, my ass.

I lean forward, elbows resting on my knees, my grin spreading. "Uh-huh. Sure. You've got no reason to be wound up, right? You and Adriana never dated or anything." I pause for effect. "It's not like there's any unresolved feelings there."

"Drop it, Gabe."

"Nah, I think I'm onto something." I can't resist poking the bear. "You and Adriana? You've always had that weird vibe going on. It's been years, but some things never change."

Julio glares, jaw tight, the muscles there working overtime. He moves to stand, but his knee knocks into the coffee table, and the sound echoes louder than I expected.

"There's no vibe," he snaps, but the way he fumbles over the words tells me otherwise.

"There's totally a vibe," I press, leaning in, my grin widening. Deacon's snickering from his side of the couch, clearly enjoying the show. "Come on, man. You've been acting weird about her for months. Ever since Cecilia brought her back into the fold."

Julio pushes to his feet, his movements jerky, almost panicked. "It's nothing." His voice wavers, though. He rubs the back of his neck, his fingers brushing over the ink of the loteria cards there. The tattooed cards and roses stretch up his throat, dark and bold, as much a part of him as his obvious irritation is right now. "And I'm not jealous, alright? Just—whatever. My bad for being concerned. She was your friend before, too. We don't know who this guy is. What if he's just some asshole looking to take advantage of her?"

I snicker, unable to help myself. "Man, you're really in your feelings. Maybe you should just tell Adriana you're interested."

Julio spins on me, dark eyes flashing. There's heat behind that look, something more than just annoyance. "Shut up, Gabe."

I throw my hands up in mock surrender. "Just sayin'. It's not that deep."

Julio doesn't respond. He storms out of the room, footsteps heavy against the hardwood, his presence gone in a matter of seconds. The door slams behind him, leaving an odd tension in the air.

Deacon leans back, a smirk still tugging at his lips. "He's totally into her, right?"

"One hundred percent," I agree, shaking my head. I grab my phone from the table, unlocking it with a swipe of my thumb. "And that fucker is definitely jealous."

Deacon chuckles. It's low, but it carries through the room, mixing with the static from the soccer game playing in the background. "What's the story there?"

"It's his to tell whenever he pulls his head out of his ass." I scroll through my texts, opening up the message from Cecilia again.

> Me: Who's the guy? Anyone I know?

Her response is immediate, like she's been waiting for me to ask.

> Cecilia: Kenji Yamada. Hockey player at PacNorth.

The name doesn't ring a bell. Not that it would. Hockey's a different world, and I've got enough guys on the soccer team to keep me busy without branching out.

> Me: K.

Cecilia: So you're in?

> Me: Sure. Sounds fun.

Since I'm not a complete asshole, I open a new chat and type out another message, this one for Julio.

> Me: Kenji Yamada. Hockey. You're welcome.

I watch as the message changes colors, letting me know he read it. No response, though. Figures.

I shrug, tossing my phone back on the table. Guess he can't say I never did him any favors.

sixteen

GABRIEL

THE WOLF DEN is buzzing with the usual Tuesday crowd—low-key but lively. College students fill the tables, pitchers of cheap beer sloshing around as they laugh too loud over the music. The air smells like fried food, beer, and a little bit of sweat. Feels like home.

I lean back, my arm draped across the back of Cecilia's chair. Her fingers trace idle patterns on my thigh, and it's doing a good job of keeping me grounded. This is what I needed. The casual vibe, the shitty beer, Cecilia close enough to touch—it's the kind of night I can sink into.

Across the table, Adriana's laughing at something Kenji just said. He's leaning back, all cocky smiles and easy charm. Typical hockey player. But, surprisingly, not a total asshole. He's got Adriana's attention, and from the way she's leaning in, I'd say she's interested.

Not my business, though. Julio's been blowing up my phone ever since I left the house, freaking out about Adriana being on this date with another guy even if he won't admit it. I shove my phone in my pocket and decide to deal with him later, but right now? Right now, I'm chilling.

"This place has changed a bit since I was here last," Kenji says, taking a pull from his beer. His eyes flick around the bar, scanning the updates. "Still has the best wings, though."

Adriana rolls her eyes, nudging him with her elbow. "You're such a guy."

He smirks. "What? A guy can appreciate good wings."

Cecilia laughs softly beside me, her eyes glancing at the menu in front of us. "Are the wings really that good?"

I chuckle. "They're decent. The burgers are better."

The conversation flows easily—light banter, quick laughs—and for the first time in a while, I feel myself relax. Cecilia's leaning into me, her shoulder brushing mine, and there's this comfortable rhythm between us tonight. After everything we've been through, this feels like a break. Like a moment to just be us, no expectations, no drama. I needed that.

Adriana catches my eye from across the table, raising an eyebrow as if she's reading my mind. She knows. She knows I'm enjoying this rare bit of peace. She flashes a smile, almost like she's telling me it's okay to let go for a bit. I forgot that about her. How well she could always read all of us.

Kenji keeps the jokes coming, pulling laughter from all of us. Turns out the guy's got more than just puck skills; he's got a great sense of humor too. Even I'm starting to warm up to the guy. I mean, he's not one of my boys, but he's not terrible to be around.

"Alright, wing challenge," Kenji announces, leaning forward with a grin. "Let's see who can handle the heat."

I snort. "Man, don't even. You'll be the first to tap out." He does realize I'm Mexican, right? There's no way some Japanese kid is going to handle heat better than I do. No offense.

Kenji raises his hands in mock defense. "Hey, if you're afraid, it's all good. I don't wanna embarrass you in front of your girl."

Challenge accepted. "You're on."

The lightheartedness is contagious. The energy at the table is good, and I catch Cecilia's smile, her eyes glowing as she leans into me. This is what it should feel like. Easy. No heaviness pressing down on my chest, no drama hanging over my head.

But then, my phone buzzes again. This time, the vibration cuts through the haze of beer and laughter. Julio. Again. The guy just won't let it go.

Cecilia glances at me, her eyes straying to my phone. "Everything okay?"

I nod, reluctantly pulling my phone from my pocket. "Yeah, all good." I discreetly skim my messages.

> Julio: So, what's up with this Kenji dude?

> Julio: Is Adriana into him? Like, for real?

He's not even trying to pretend at this point. My boy's got it bad.

> Julio: You'd tell me if she was, right?

Julio: I mean, I'm not saying I care, but ... don't you think it's weird she said yes to going out with some random guy? Doesn't she realize how dangerous that is?

Julio: You should tell her how dangerous it is. She can't just agree to meet up with complete strangers.

Julio: Hey! Cabrón. Answer me.

He needs to take a serious chill pill. I'm betting he's pacing the house right now, probably trying to decide whether or not to crash our date. Fucking hell.

Me: Chill the fuck out. It's not dangerous. I'm here. Now go do something because I'm turning my phone off.

I drop the phone face down on the table, out of sight, out of mind.

"All good?" Cecilia's eyes are soft, concerned, but I wave it off.

"Yeah, just Julio being ... Julio." I shrug. "He'll get over it."

Cecilia's fingers tighten on my leg, her smile reassuring. I lean in and capture her lips in a quick kiss. "I like this," I tell her.

"Double dates?" she teases.

I shrug. "Just ... being with you."

She opens her mouth to reply but before she does, I catch movement out of the corner of my eye. A guy stands at the edge of our table, his presence casting a shadow over our group.

"Gabriel?"

Hearing my name drags my attention from Cecilia, and when I glance up, the easy vibe of the night shatters. I recognize who he is right away. Adam. As in, my brand-new stepbrother, Adam.

"Hey man," Kenji greets the newcomer with a smile. "What are you doing here?"

Adam hesitates, his eyes flicking back over to me. "Uhh—"

"You two know each other?" I ask.

"Of course," Kenji says. "Mouse is our goalie. He plays for PacNorth, too."

"Mouse?"

Kenji's smile widens, and Adam's face turns beet red.

"Yeah, it's his name on the ice. Adam here is quiet like a mouse. You never know where he's at until he's all but on top of you." Kenji chuckles, clearly not sensing the new tension in the room. "How do you two know each other?"

I give Adam a pointed look, and when it's obvious he's not going to answer his teammate, I do it for him. "We don't," I tell him.

Adam shifts his weight, glancing at Cecilia before meeting my eyes again. "Sorry. I didn't mean to interrupt your evening. We haven't really talked since ... well, the wedding." He rubs the back of his neck. "I was sort of hoping we could clear the air."

Right. The wedding. The shitshow where I realized my Mom found replacements for the entire lot of us.

This guy wants to clear the air? Tough. There's nothing to say.

I feel Cecilia shift beside me, her hand tensing on my knee. She's waiting to see how I'll react, so for her sake, I grit my teeth and force myself to lean back in my seat. "Nothing to clear," I tell him.

Adam's mouth tightens, his voice a little softer now, like he's walking on glass. "I just wanted to say I'm sorry. About all of it. I didn't mean to cause any problems for you."

I grind my teeth together. I can't deal with this. He's standing there looking like a kicked puppy, and all I can think about is how my mom's got this shiny new family. I don't need another brother. I had one. He's dead. And Adam? He's just a reminder of everything I don't have. A reminder I definitely do not need.

"It's fine," I say, even though it's not. My voice comes out colder than I mean it to, but I don't care. "Don't worry about it."

Adam doesn't move. His eyes flick to Kenji like he's waiting for a lifeline.

Kenji notices. He leans back, tossing his arm over the back of his chair like he owns the place. "Terrific! So everyone is good now." He gives Adam a smile, then looks at me. "Adam and I know each other from middle school. We've played hockey together for what?" He pretends to count in his head. "Seven years now. The kid's solid." I catch what he's not saying out loud. He and Adam are friends. Close enough that he's got his back should I decide to start anything. Not that I planned to. But I hear his message loud and clear and dip my chin to acknowledge it.

"I'm sure he is," I tell him. "But like I said, we don't really know one another." Nothing to see here. Can we please move this shit along?

148

Adam clears his throat again, looking back at me. "I just wanted to clear the air. I heard what you said at the wedding and ... I'm not trying to replace anyone. I just ... I wanted to apologize and let you know that uh, I'm here. If you ever want to hang out or ... you know. Whatever. I'm around."

And there it is. That offer. It's almost laughable. I tighten my grip around the beer in my hand and force my features into an expressionless mask.

"My brother died," I tell him, raising the bottle to my lips. "Unlike my mother, I'm not looking for any replacements."

The words hang between us, cold and final. Adam's face falls a little. He doesn't push it, though. Doesn't try to argue or make excuses. He just nods, taking the hit, like he was expecting this all along.

"Alright. Well, if you change your mind, I'll be around."

Kenji's eyes flick between us, but he's smart enough not to say anything. He gives Adam a quick nod. "We'll catch up later, yeah?"

Adam manages a weak smile and walks away. I watch him go, his shoulders tight, like he's carrying around a weight I didn't ask him to. The bar feels ten degrees hotter now, the noise from the crowd turning into a low hum of irritation in my skull. I can feel Cecilia watching me, but I can't look at her right now. I can't look at anything but the door and Adam's back as he slowly walks away.

"You okay?" Cecilia's hand is still on my knee, but her grip is different now—tighter, worried.

I take a long sip of my drink, letting the burn settle in my chest. "Yeah. I'm fine."

Lie.

The rest of the night goes by in a blur. Adriana and Kenji hit it off and Cecilia joins in their conversation. We order a round of burgers and wings, and Kenji and I both have a few more beers. I keep waiting for the tight feeling in my chest to lessen, but despite the hour that passes, it never really does.

"You okay?" Cecilia asks after Kenji gets up to use the bathroom.

"All good," I tell her with a grin.

"Don't do that," Adriana interjects. "She doesn't deserve your lies."

My mouth tightens. "Now isn't really the—"

"Yes, it is," she interrupts me again. "Whatever it is about him, that kid got in your head. You've given tonight a solid effort. Kudos. I'm proud of you. But get your head out of your ass. Go home and talk about your feelings with your girl. I'll tell Kenji you guys decided to call it a night while you go get your head on straight."

My knee-jerk reaction is to snap at her, but as her words settle over me, it dawns on me that she's actually doing me a favor. Pulling my wallet out, I toss a few bills on the table to cover mine and Cecilia's tab and then I tug my girl to her feet.

"Thank you," I say to Adriana.

She gives me a two-fingered salute. "It's what I'm here for," she says. To Cecilia she adds, "Make him talk to you. Don't let him bury all this shit down. Okay?"

"I won't."

With that, we make our way outside. Cecilia slides her arm around my waist, leaning into me as we walk toward her Jeep. "I'm sorry about tonight."

I press a quick kiss to her temple, trying to push the guilt down. "You don't have anything to be sorry about," I tell her. "I had a good time." But as the cold air bites at my skin, I know I'm lying. Because tonight stirred up shit I've been trying to avoid, and now I have no idea how to deal with it.

seventeen
CECILIA

THE DRIVE back to Gabriel's place is quiet, the tension between us thick like a weight pressing into my chest. He's staring out the window, jaw clenched, his fingers tapping a beat against his thigh, a rhythm that doesn't match the calm I'm trying to find in the silence.

I should say something. Anything. Ask if he's okay. But I already know he's not. He's drowning, and I'm stuck on the shore, wondering how to pull him out.

As we pull up in front of his house, I shift in the driver's seat, fingers gripping the steering wheel like it'll stop the nervous energy buzzing in my veins. "I can head home if you need space," I offer, my voice softer than I mean it to be, trying to gauge his mood.

I expect him to say yes. Take the out. But instead, he surprises me.

"No. Stay." Gabriel's voice is rough, low, cutting through the silence. His hand finds mine, resting on my thigh, fingers brushing over the denim like he's holding onto me for balance. "Please."

My heart stutters. There's something in his eyes—something desperate, a plea wrapped in all that tension.

"Of course," I whisper, squeezing his hand.

We get out of the Jeep, the night air biting at my skin as we make our way to the front door. Gabriel unlocks it, and we step inside. The house is dim, quiet except for the low hum of the refrigerator. But before we can get upstairs, Julio's voice slices through the silence.

"Where's Adriana?"

Gabriel sighs, his shoulders sagging as he turns toward his roommate. Julio stands in the kitchen doorway, arms crossed, eyes sharp with something close to rage. I don't think I've ever seen him this upset before. He's normally the calm, level-headed one in their bunch.

"She's still out with Kenji," Gabriel says, his tone clipped like he doesn't have the energy for this conversation. Not tonight.

Julio's jaw tightens, the vein in his neck pulsing against his colorful tattoos. "You left her with him? Alone?"

"She's fine, man," Gabriel mutters, running a hand through his hair. "She's a grown-ass woman. She doesn't need a babysitter."

Julio grabs his keys off the counter, snatches up his motorcycle helmet, and storms past us, muttering under his breath. "I'm going to check on her."

Gabriel doesn't stop him. Just watches as Julio disappears out the door, the sound of his bike roaring to life seconds later.

I glance at Gabriel, worry creeping into my chest. "Should I warn her?"

"Nah," he says, rubbing the back of his neck. "He might come to his senses on his way there, and if not ..." He shrugs. "She knows how to handle him. Julio's just ..." He trails off, not finishing the thought, but I know what he's thinking. There's something brewing between those two, and I don't want to be in the middle of it when things finally come to a head.

"If he causes a scene, I'm sure I'll hear about it later."

Gabriel grunts and then motions toward the hall. "Come on."

I follow him upstairs, my steps light, but the weight in the air between us is heavy. The door shuts behind us, and the stillness thickens. I sit on the edge of the bed, fiddling with my sleeve, unsure if I should say something. I pushed Gabriel to deal with his feelings before, and it blew up in my face. I'm not making that mistake again.

He paces the room, hands dragging through his hair, his frustration radiating off him in waves. It's like he's searching for a fight that won't come.

"I know Adam's not the enemy," he finally says, his voice strained like it's costing him something to admit it. "He didn't do anything wrong. Hell, he's just trying to be nice. But I fucking hate him anyway."

I stay quiet, letting him talk. His muscles are tight, his jaw clenched so hard I can almost hear his teeth grinding.

"He's who she replaced us with, you know? Me. Carlos." His voice cracks on his brother's name, and my heart twists in my chest.

155

Gabriel stops pacing, his eyes locking on mine, raw and exposed. "I'm an asshole, Cecilia. I know that. He didn't ask for any of this. But every time I see him, it's like he's taking what's mine. What's supposed to be mine."

I stand up, closing the space between us. My fingers brush his arm, trying to anchor him. "It's okay to feel that way, Gabriel. To be angry. Your feelings don't have to make sense. Not to anyone else. And you don't owe Adam a relationship just because he wants one."

His eyes flicker, the storm in them softening just enough. "I know. But fuck, I don't know how to let go of it."

"You don't have to. Not yet." My voice is quiet, but firm. "You'll figure it out when you're ready."

Gabriel's hand cups the back of my neck, pulling me close until our foreheads touch, his breath warm against my lips. "Thank you," he whispers, his voice rough. "For being here. For understanding."

Before I can respond, his lips crash into mine, rough and desperate, like he needs this. Needs me. It's not just a kiss—it's a claiming, and I melt into him, my hands gripping his shirt as I kiss him back with the same hunger.

He doesn't slow down. His hands slide to my waist, fingers digging into my skin as he lifts me, my legs wrapping around his hips as he carries me to the bed, the heat between us growing hotter by the second.

I know we were supposed to take things slow. We promised. But right now? Right now, I don't give a damn.

"Fuck, you're perfect," Gabriel growls against my throat, his hands tugging my shirt over my head. His voice is low, possessive, like he's staking his claim on every inch of me. "I don't deserve you, but I'm keeping you anyway."

"Don't say that." I don't know how I manage to get the words out between the way he's touching me, his fingers brushing over my skin like I'm his lifeline. "Of course, you do."

His lips crash into mine again, harder this time, his hands working my jeans free. "I need you naked. Now." His command sends a rush of heat through me, and I'm quick to help him strip off the rest of my clothes.

"Fuck, Cecilia," he says my name like a plea. "You're fucking perfect."

The way he looks at me—like he's devouring me with his eyes— makes me shiver. His eyes darken as he drinks me in, his expression growing hungrier by the second.

"Gabriel?" I ask when all he does is continue to stare.

My voice must snap him out of his reverie because the next thing I know, he's stripping off his own clothes, each piece falling to the floor with a newfound sense of urgency.

I only have a few seconds to take in the rigid lines of his abdomen and his thick, muscular thighs before he's on me again —his body pressing mine into the mattress, his lips claiming mine as if it's the only thing keeping him alive.

It doesn't take long before I'm drowning in him, my mind spinning, dizzy with desire.

"Gabriel," I gasp, my hands clutching at his back, pulling him closer. I want this. I want him. And I don't care about anything else.

"God, I want you." His voice is rough, his breath hot against my ear as his hand slides between my thighs, teasing me with just enough pressure to make me gasp. "Tell me you want this. Want me."

"Yes," I breathe, my voice trembling with need. As if I could ever deny him. "Always."

"Mine." He growls against my skin, his fingers working me into a frenzy, his touch possessive and sure. And when I come apart in his hands, I know with absolute certainty that this is where I belong. I was an idiot for ever thinking we needed to take things slow.

Gabriel's lips trail fire down my neck, each kiss pulling a shaky breath from my chest as I come down from my release. His hands are everywhere—rough palms tracing the curve of my hips, sliding over my thighs, leaving a path of heat in their wake. I shudder beneath him, the world narrowing to the feel of his skin on mine, the weight of his body pressing me into the bed.

"Cecilia ..." he groans, his voice thick and strained as if he's barely holding himself together. There's something raw about the way he looks at me now, like I'm the only thing keeping him from unraveling.

His lips find mine again, hungry and demanding, and I meet his kiss with the same intensity, my body arching into his. I can't think straight, can't focus on anything but the feel of him, the way his breath hitches when I run my hands down his chest. I'm desperate—aching—for more. I need him inside of me. I need ... fuck. I can't think.

"Tell me what you need," he growls, pulling back just enough for his dark eyes to burn into mine, the heat in his gaze making my heart race. His thumb brushes over my lower lip, and I feel like I'm coming undone under the weight of his stare.

"I need you," I whisper, breathless, my voice barely more than a plea. I don't recognize this version of myself—the one who's willing to beg. But for him? For Gabriel, I'd happily get down on my knees. "Please," I gasp. "I need you inside me."

He growls again, low in his throat, before his hands slide down to my thighs, spreading them open, his gaze never leaving mine. "Fuck, baby," he breathes, his chin dropping down to his chest. "We said slow but ..." he curses.

My body thrums with anticipation. "I don't want slow," I tell him. "I want you. I want this, Gabriel. Please."

That's all it takes to break the last of his control.

In one swift motion, he's baring down on me, his length lining up between my thighs, his lips crashing down on my mouth in a kiss that steals the air from my lungs. I clutch at his back, nails digging into his skin, desperate to hold on to something—anything—as he moves against me. As he sinks inch after torturous inch into my dripping entrance.

Every touch is electric, every kiss is fire, and I feel like I'm about to burst, the tension between us coiling tighter and tighter until it feels like I might snap. His name slips from my lips, a soft moan that seems to drive him wild. His hands grip my hips as he moves faster, harder, his breath hot against my ear.

I'm lost in him, completely undone, my body shaking as the pleasure builds and builds until it's too much, until I'm falling apart beneath him all over again. My mind is spinning, my heart racing, and his name is the only thing I can think, the only word I can say.

"Gabriel!" In one perfect, overwhelming moment, I shatter.

His hands hold me steady, grounding me as the pleasure washes over me, wave after wave.

But he doesn't stop.

He moves against me with the same intensity, his lips tracing the curve of my neck, biting down just enough to make me arch into him. The rhythm of his hips is steady, relentless, dragging me higher and higher again, even though I feel like I've already given him everything I have.

"Fuck," he growls against my skin, his voice thick, almost desperate. "Cecilia ... you have no idea what you do to me."

I can barely think, let alone speak. The sound of his voice—raw, strained, full of need—pushes me toward the edge again. *Oh god. I can't. No. It's too much.*

My nails dig into his back, the ache in me building all over again until every inch of me is begging for release. I'm dizzy, lost in the feel of him, the weight of him above me, the way his body moves with mine like we were made for one another.

He lifts his head, his eyes locking with mine. His gaze is dark, intense, filled with something deeper than just lust. There's a raw vulnerability there, a look that makes my chest tighten, my heart twist. He's not just taking me; he's giving himself to me, in a way I wasn't expecting.

"I need you," he whispers, his forehead resting against mine. "I fucking need you, *mi sueña.*"

The words hit me harder than they should. I don't know if it's the heat of the moment, the way his voice shakes, or the weight behind them, but something about the way he says it makes me feel like I'm falling. Like this is more than just sex. More than just desire. It's everything.

I don't answer him with words. Instead, I pull him closer, wrapping my legs around his waist, urging him deeper. My hands slide up to tangle in his hair, and I kiss him like he's the only thing keeping me anchored to the earth.

He groans into my mouth, his body tensing as he pushes harder, faster. The friction is almost too much, my body burning with the overwhelming intensity of it all, and I feel that familiar tension coil in my stomach, tighter and tighter, ready to snap.

"That's it. One more. Give me one more, baby," he growls against my lips as one hand slips down between my thighs. Gabriel doesn't miss a beat as he continues to thrust into me while his fingers circle my swollen clit. And within seconds, I fall apart in his arms all over again. Completely undone.

Gabriel is right behind me, his body shuddering as he buries his nose in the crook of my neck. His breath is hot and ragged against my skin. And his hips jerk one final time before I feel the hot spurts of his release.

For a moment, the world is still. Quiet, except for the sound of our breathing, heavy and uneven. Gabriel doesn't move at first. He doesn't pull away. Instead, he stays there, his weight comforting, his arms wrapped around me like he's afraid to let go.

I close my eyes, letting myself sink into the warmth of him, the feel of his heartbeat slowly evening out against my chest.

"That was ...." He trails off, breathing heavily.

"Yeah. It was." There's a smile in my voice I don't bother to hide.

With a quick kiss, Gabriel rolls off of me, his arms taking me with him and nestling my body into his side. "Thank you," he murmurs, voice thick with exhaustion.

"For what? The orgasm?" I tease, poking at his side.

He flinches away with a smile that lets me know I found a ticklish spot. I might need to explore that another time. Maybe when I have more energy.

"No, you brat," he admonishes but without any heat. "For being you. For ..." He sighs, the sound filled with contentment. "For being exactly what I need."

eighteen

GABRIEL

THE CLANG of lockers shutting echoes behind me as I walk out of the locker room, my bag slung over my shoulder. Sweat still clings to my skin, the burn of practice fresh in my muscles. I run a hand through my damp hair, catching sight of my boys just ahead. Atticus is laughing at something Felix said, probably something dumb, knowing him. Julio's already got his helmet in hand, dark tattoos standing out against the sleeves of his shirt as he talks with Deacon.

It's routine—practice, a little shit-talking, then the ride back to the soccer house. It's comfortable. Predictable. And right now, predictable is what I need.

"Hey, G, you coming, or you planning to hang back and stare at us all day?" Atticus throws a grin over his shoulder, tossing his bag in the back of his car. With that white-blond hair and baby face, he looks more like a Slytherin reject than the PacNorth's rising star goalie, but somehow, he still holds his own with our crew.

Felix follows his lead, brown hair tousled and messy, always with that laid-back vibe like he's never stressed a day in his life.

I roll my eyes and give him a middle finger, dropping my own bag next to my Honda CBR 1000, matte black and sleek as hell. The sound of it starting up is like a second heartbeat to me —steady, grounding.

Julio swings his leg over his bike, and Deacon and Atticus are still cracking jokes by the car, but I can't seem to shake this feeling. There's an itch between my shoulders. That inexplicable feeling someone else is out here.

That's when I spot him.

Stepbrother number two.

Fuck.

He's heading my way, his face set with purpose. My mood sours instantly, the easy camaraderie with the guys disappearing as quickly as it came. Great. The last thing I need right now is another unwanted chat with mine and Carlos's replacements.

"See you back at the house?" Atticus calls out, the guys already starting to pile into the car or onto their bikes. Felix gives me a quick wave, and Julio shoots me a look like *you good?* before they rev their engines and pull out.

I nod, even though I'm low-key pissed they're leaving me to deal with this alone.

Asher slows when he gets close, his expression somewhere between cautious and annoyed. Great. He doesn't even want to be here either. So why are we doing this?

"Heard you talked to Adam the other night," Asher starts, his voice low, careful, like he's trying not to set me off. "He came home pretty torn up about it."

My jaw clenches. Of course, he did. I shake my head, pushing down the anger rising up inside me. What, did he think I was going to roll out the welcome mat?

"We talked," I confirm. "We're cool." I'm lying through my teeth. Inside, I'm pissed. These guys keep trying to drop into my life, but I'm not interested in being part of their shiny new family. I've got my own shit to deal with, and I sure as hell don't need them complicating it. Is it too much to ask to be left the fuck alone?

I can tell from the way Asher's jaw ticks that he doesn't believe me. His arms cross, brown eyes locking on mine. There's a challenge there, just beneath the surface. "Look, I'm not here to push for anything between us. We don't need to be brothers or even friends. But Adam? He's hurting. He knows he messed up, and he just wants to fix things with you."

Fix things? There's nothing to fix because there was nothing there to begin with. My chest tightens. Adam didn't do anything wrong, he's just another reminder that my real brother is gone.

I keep my face neutral, but inside, I'm fighting the urge to roll my eyes. "There's nothing to fix," I say, my voice sharper than I intended. "We're good."

Asher's gaze hardens, an edge creeping into his tone. "Look, Gabriel. You had a brother before. I get it. I'm sorry he's dead. But if you were in my shoes, you'd be doing the same thing. Adam is a good kid, man. He's got a soft heart, and he won't be able to let this go until he knows things are okay between you two."

I bite the inside of my cheek, the words hitting harder than they should. Asher's watching me closely, like he's waiting for something to crack. And maybe it is. Maybe that mention of Carlos, my brother, my other half—it's enough to make me pause.

"You don't have to like him," Asher continues, his voice softer now, less combative. "But can you at least try not to be an asshole? For him? He's my kid brother. I've got to look out for him."

I let out a long breath, my chest tight. He's tugging on shit I don't want to think about. Guilt twisting in a way that's impossible to ignore. "Fine," I say, finally meeting his gaze. "If I see Adam around, I'll be cordial."

It's a weak concession, but it's all I've got.

Asher nods, relief flashing in his eyes. "I appreciate it."

I grunt. I'd love for this conversation to end here, but he's still standing in front of me like he's working up to say something else.

"So, uh." He rubs the back of his neck, his expression sheepish. "I heard the Wolves have a game coming up."

I nod. "Yeah. Next weekend against Suncrest U." Where is he going with this?

His lips press together, and he shifts on his feet, clearly uncomfortable. "Would you mind if we ... I don't know, maybe, grabbed a beer after the game?"

Oh, fuck no. I open my mouth to shut that down, but he barrels on.

"You can bring some of your teammates," he adds, his tone almost desperate now. "Doesn't need to be anything weird. Just ... casual. Adam just wants a chance to hang out. That's all."

I want to tell him to fuck off. To tell him and Adam both to leave me alone. But something in his eyes—something about the way he's trying so damn hard for his brother—makes me pause.

He must see the hesitation because he's quick to follow up. "You don't have to commit right now. I'll give you my number. If you decide it's cool, just let me know. No pressure, yeah?"

I sigh, running a hand through my hair. "Fine. Whatever." I pull out my phone and punch in his number, more out of obligation than any real intent to use it.

"Cool." He nods, clearly relieved. "We'll see you at the game."

He turns and walks away, leaving me standing there alone with the heaviness of a conversation I didn't want to have.

I swing my leg over the bike, the weight of the helmet in my hand feeling heavier than usual. I don't want to be a dick to these guys. But fuck, I don't know how to let them in.

nineteen

CECILIA

THE CURSOR BLINKS on my laptop screen, the words from my online homework assignment blurring together as my mind drifts.

I can't seem to focus today.

I keep replaying our date at The Wolf Den two nights ago, how tense Gabriel was after talking to Adam. He hasn't mentioned it since, and I haven't pushed, but it's been gnawing at me.

I sigh, rubbing my temples just as I hear my mom call from downstairs.

"Cecilia, you have a visitor!"

I frown, pushing away from my desk. The tone in her voice is—excited. I head downstairs, the soft creak of the stairs beneath my feet the only sound breaking the silence. When I reach the bottom, I pause. My mom is standing in the doorway, her eyes flicking between me and the porch.

"Guess who's here?" she says with a wide grin as she steps aside.

Gabriel stands on the front porch, one hand in his pocket, the other holding onto his helmet. His eyes are shadowed with something I can't quite place. He looks exhausted, worn out, like something's pulling him under, and not for the first time today, my stomach tightens with worry.

I thought we were meeting later tonight?

"Gabriel ..." His name barely makes it past my lips.

My mom senses the weight of the moment and offers a small, understanding smile. "I'll give you two some privacy." She disappears into the kitchen, leaving us alone.

Gabriel steps forward, his mouth bracketed with strain, but before I can ask what's wrong, he speaks. "Can you come out with me? Please. I know it's early but ..."

It's the "please" that gets me. It's clipped, heavy, like he's holding onto something he can't control. I don't ask questions. I don't need to. I just nod. "Give me a second."

I rush back upstairs, grabbing my shoes and the first sweater I find, my heart thudding in my chest. I don't know what's going on, but whatever it is, it's eating at him.

When I return to the porch, Gabriel's still there, leaning against the railing. The weight in his posture tells me more than any words could right now. He hands me his helmet, the familiar shadow of the matte black visor swallowing the light.

"Here," he says, his voice quiet.

I take the helmet, slip it on, and follow him to his bike. The engine roars to life as I climb on behind him, my arms wrapping around his waist. The leather of his jacket is cool under my fingers, the solid warmth of his body grounding me.

We take off down the street, the wind whipping against my face, the sound of the bike drowning out everything else. Gabriel drives like he's got nowhere to be, weaving through the streets of Richland with no real destination in mind. I can feel the tension in his body, the way his muscles tighten every time we stop at a light, how he grips the handlebars like he's holding on for dear life.

My worry grows with each mile. Something's bothering him, gnawing at him, but I know him well enough to know he's not ready to talk about it. Not yet. Right now I'm just grateful he came and got me. This is his way of letting me in.

Twenty minutes pass, having taken the scenic route, before we pull up in front of his place. I take off the helmet, my hair a tangled mess, but I don't care. I slide off the bike, watching as Gabriel gets off slowly, like the burden of whatever's on his mind is dragging him down.

"Come on," he says, his voice low.

He reaches out for my hand, and I place my palm in his before following him up the porch steps.

The house is quiet, but I doubt it's empty. The guys are probably all just in their rooms or maybe hanging out back. Gabriel heads to the living room, flicks on the TV, and then drops onto the sofa, tugging me down with him, "Wanna watch a movie?"

It's a distraction. A way to fill the silence without having to talk, but I agree anyway. "Sure."

We sit on the couch, side by side, but Gabriel's stiff. He's trying to act normal, but I can feel it—the tension radiating off him, the way his leg bounces slightly, how his arms are folded tight across his chest. His mind is somewhere else, miles away from me and this living room.

I glance at him, my chest aching for him. What the hell happened today to make him like this?

Gently, I reach out, my fingers slipping beneath the hem of his shirt. I trace the hard lines of his abdomen, the ridges of muscle warm under my touch. He sucks in a sharp breath, his body going still, and when he turns to look at me, his gaze is heated, intense. The storm in his eyes shifts, turning from frustration to something darker, something desperate.

Suddenly, the tension in the room morphs into something heavier. There's this charge in the air now.

Gabriel moves fast, his lips crashing into mine with a desperation that makes my heart race. He kisses me like he's starving for something only I can give him, and I melt into it, my hands fisting his shirt, pulling him closer. His fingers are in my hair, his touch rough and possessive as he deepens the kiss, his tongue sweeping across mine in a way that sends heat spiraling through me.

Before I know it, I'm straddling his lap, my knees on either side of his hips, grinding down against him. He groans into my mouth, his hands sliding up my thighs, gripping me tight. His hips thrust up to meet mine, the friction between us electric, every movement sending a jolt of pleasure through my body.

My breath is coming in short gasps, my heart pounding in my chest. I can feel him, hard and ready beneath me, and a thrill shoots through me, my body reacting without thought. But just as I lose myself in the heat of it, a thought slams into me like a cold bucket of water.

Gabriel doesn't live alone. *Shit.*

I pull back, my chest heaving as I meet his gaze. His pupils are blown wide, his breathing just as ragged as mine. He frowns, confusion etched into his face.

"We ... we should go upstairs," I whisper, my voice hoarse, my cheeks flaming.

Gabriel blinks, processing my words, then a slow, wicked grin spreads across his face. "Yeah, we should," he murmurs, his hands sliding to my waist. He lifts me off his lap, standing and pulling me with him.

"Let's get out of here before someone walks in," he adds, his voice low and rough with desire.

I don't argue. My heart's still racing, my body thrumming with the need for more.

The second we're locked behind his bedroom door, something snaps inside Gabriel.

He spins me around, pressing me up against the cool wood, his body flush against mine. His hands grip my hips, firm and unyielding, and his lips are back on mine, kissing me with a hunger that steals the breath right from my lungs. There's no hesitation, no gentleness—just raw need. His urgency is all-consuming and desperate, the heat of his body searing through my clothes.

The tension that's been building between us finally snaps, and it's like a dam breaking, all of that frustration pouring into the way he touches me.

"Fuck, baby," he growls against my lips, his breath hot and ragged as his fingers slip beneath my sweater, pushing it up over my head. The material hits the floor, forgotten, and his hands are everywhere—roaming over my skin, leaving a trail of fire in their wake. He's rougher than usual, and I feel it in every touch, every graze of his fingertips, as if he's no longer treating me with kid gloves.

Every brush of his hands against my skin feels electric, each touch sending shivers straight to my core.

I shudder under his touch, my heart pounding in my chest. He's overwhelming in the best way, his body, his presence, all-consuming. There's an intensity I haven't felt from him before, something raw, unchecked, like he's done holding back.

I can feel his heartbeat hammering in sync with mine, the heat rolling off him in waves. I reach for his shirt, tugging at the hem, desperate to feel his skin against mine.

Gabriel rips his shirt off, the movement quick and rough, like he can't stand the distance between us for a second more.

And then he's on me again, his hands cupping my face as his mouth moves against mine. I sink into it, into him, my fingers digging into the hard lines of his shoulders as I arch into his touch, needing more.

Gabriel's hands slide down my sides, gripping the waistband of my jeans. With a quick flick, he unbuttons them, pushing them down over my hips in one swift motion. I kick them off, my skin already buzzing with anticipation. But the way he moves, there's no softness, only possessiveness—like I'm something he needs to claim and mark.

He pulls back just enough to look at me, his eyes dark, filled with raw desire. "God. You're perfect," he whispers, his voice thick with hunger, almost reverent, like he's seeing me for the first time. His fingers trace the edge of my panties, teasing, and I gasp, my body arching toward him.

"Gabriel," I sigh, my voice breathy.

He smirks, his lips brushing the sensitive skin of my neck, sending shivers down my spine. "Tell me what you need, baby." His voice is a low growl, his breath hot against my ear as his fingers dip lower, teasing me through the fabric.

"I need you," I gasp, my hands clutching at his arms, my short nails digging into his skin. "I need more."

His grip tightens on my hips, the bruising pressure unmistakable, but I don't care. I want this side of him.

"That's my girl," he murmurs, his lips trailing down the column of my throat, kissing, biting, sucking, until my head falls back against the door, a moan slipping from my lips. His teeth scrape against my skin, rougher than before, and it sends a spark of heat straight to my core.

With one swift motion, he yanks my panties down, tossing them aside, and then his fingers are on me, sliding between my thighs, teasing the heat of my core. I'm trembling, my breath coming in quick bursts as his fingers find the slickness between my legs. I whimper. His touch sends sparks of pleasure shooting through me.

"You're so fucking wet," he groans, his breath hot against my skin. "This all for me?"

I can barely respond, my breath coming in short gasps as his fingers work me into a frenzy, each stroke pulling me closer and closer to the edge. My legs feel weak, my body shaking, but Gabriel's there, his other arm wrapped around my waist, holding me steady. His grip is firm, controlling, and I'm at his mercy, falling apart under his touch.

"Please," I beg, my voice barely more than a whisper. "I need you, Gabriel.

His eyes darken, something dangerous flickering in their depths, and in one swift movement, he lifts me off the ground, carrying me like I weigh nothing.

My back hits the mattress, and he's over me, his lips devouring mine. His hands are everywhere, rough and demanding, and I can feel the hardness of him pressing against me, thick and ready between the material of his jeans.

"Tell me you're mine," he growls, his voice rough, his lips bruising.

"I'm yours," I breathe, arching up into him, my hands fisting in his hair. "I've always been yours."

That's all it takes.

Gabriel shoves down his jeans and underwear before positioning himself between my thighs. His movements are rough, impatient, as if he can't stand the wait any longer. "You want me to fuck you?" he asks.

Hearing him ask it like that, it causes butterflies to explode in my stomach because yes, I'd very much like for him to fuck me right now.

"Yes. Please."

In one smooth thrust, he fills me completely. There's no hesitation, no slowness—just raw, unfiltered need. The air leaves my lungs, a strangled moan slipping out as my body adjusts to the stretch. My back arches off the bed, the sensation overwhelming, but so, so good. He stills for a moment, his forehead pressing against mine, both of us breathing hard.

"Fuck," he groans, his voice strained, his breath hot against my skin. "You feel so fucking good. Your pussy squeezing my cock."

I can't speak, can't think. All I can do is feel—every inch of him inside me, the way he stretches me, fills me, consumes me. There's no tenderness in his thrusts. They're rough, demanding, pushing me to the edge faster than I thought possible.

His steady pace becomes something more urgent, more desperate, and Gabriel's thrusts get even harder, faster. His fingers dig into my hips, his breaths coming faster, rougher, like he's losing control. With each snap of his hips, it's as if he's trying to imprint himself on me.

"Gabriel!" I moan, my nails digging into his back, desperate for something to hold onto. The pleasure builds and builds until I can't take it anymore.

His hand wraps around my neck, taking me by surprise. My eyes widen and his fingers apply just enough pressure for the adrenaline to kick in.

I gasp.

His eyes lock on mine. "Come for me, baby," he growls, his eyes never straying. "Let go. Let me feel your pussy strangle my dick."

And I do.

I come undone, the tension in my body snapping all at once, pleasure crashing through me in waves so intense I can't even scream.

My orgasm rips through me, my body shaking, trembling beneath him as wave after wave of pleasure crashes over me. Gabriel isn't far behind, his movements becoming frantic, desperate, and then he's groaning my name, his body tensing as he finds his own release.

For a moment, everything is still, quiet except for the sound of our breathing, heavy and uneven. Gabriel stays there, his body pressed against mine, his weight comforting.

He shudders, and I close my eyes, sinking into the warmth of him, the feel of his heartbeat evening out against my chest. My hands lift, fingers running through his hair.

"I've got you," I tell him. Letting him know I'm here. Whenever he's ready to talk. I'm right here.

twenty

GABRIEL

THE MOMENT I pull out from between Cecilia's thighs, a flood of satisfaction and exhaustion rolls over me. My breath is ragged, her skin warm beneath my hands. I should go to the bathroom, grab a warm wash rag and help her clean up.

But something in me twists at the idea, this primal urge tightening in my chest. Before I can think it through, I shove two fingers into her dripping entrance, pushing my cum back inside her.

Cecilia gasps, her body jerking under my touch. "What ... what are you doing?"

I glance down at her, the words slipping from my lips before I even realize what I'm saying. "I'm plugging you up."

Her breath hitches, dark brown eyes widening as she stares at me. "Why?"

My brows furrow. *Why?* Hell, I don't know. It's something I *needed* to do. My fingers stay buried inside her, her core tight around them. I meet her gaze, my voice gravelly. "I don't know. Just ... felt right."

She swallows hard, her chest rising and falling with each shallow breath, and I can see the questions spinning in her head, her body tensing beneath me. So, I ask her something I've never really considered before, until now. "Have you ever thought about kids?"

Her eyes flicker in surprise, but she nods after a beat. "Yeah, I mean ... I think I'll have some eventually. Not right now. I'm still in school, and ... we're still figuring things out." Her cheeks pink. Good. She's not only thought about having kids, but has specifically thought about having them with me.

Her words make sense. I've got college and soccer to think about too. But there's this part of me that doesn't care about the timeline. The thought of her growing round with my child, carrying something we made together ... it does something to me.

I lean down, brushing my lips against her forehead, then her cheeks, and finally her mouth, kissing away the worry that lingers in her expression. "I'm not suggesting you get pregnant right now," I murmur, my breath mingling with hers. "But I like the idea of you ... growing round with my baby."

She laughs softly, though it's a little shaky. "I'm on the pill, Gabriel."

I shrug, a slow smile spreading across my face as I pull back just enough to look into her eyes. "That's fine. I still like the idea of my cum staying inside you."

Her lips part, a small breath escaping, her body shifting beneath me as my words settle in. I see it, the way her body responds even though we've just come down from the high.

"I want you to keep it," I tell her. "Don't wash me away."

She bites her lip, and a pretty blush creeps up her neck. "Okay ... I won't wash you off. Not right now, at least."

Satisfaction blooms deep inside me at her words. My chest tightens with possessiveness, my lips pressing to her temple as we settle into the bed. I keep her close, her body tucked against mine like she's meant to be there. Her fingers trace slow, lazy circles on my chest, grounding me, easing the tension that still hums beneath my skin.

The silence between us stretches on, but it's not uncomfortable. Heavy with everything unsaid, but I can feel her *thinking*. I can feel her wanting to ask, but she waits.

Eventually, she shifts slightly, her voice soft, careful. "Do you want to talk about earlier? You don't have to, but ... you've been off since you picked me up."

I let out a long breath, my fingers running through her hair as I stare up at the ceiling. "I ran into Asher," I say, voice gruff. "He wants me to be nice to Adam. Maybe even grab a beer with them after the game next weekend."

She stills for a moment, her fingers pausing mid-circle on my chest before she lifts her head to look at me. "How do you feel about that?"

I shrug, the frustration simmering just below the surface starting to bubble over. "I don't know, Cecilia. I don't know how I'm supposed to feel. Part of me wants to tell him to fuck off. The other part can't stop thinking about Carlos." My brother's ghost is everywhere these days. No matter how much I try to shove it down, I can't shake the guilt, the ache. I thought I was getting good at burying his ghost but lately, I guess not.

Her hand slides up to cup my jaw, guiding my face toward hers. "They're not replacing Carlos, Gabriel. They couldn't, even if they tried. But you've lost a lot of family, and if they're reaching out ... maybe it's not the worst thing to have more people in your corner."

I let her words sink in, the tension in my chest loosening just a bit. She's right. She usually is. But it's hard, letting down my guard after losing so much. I exhale slowly, nodding against her palm. "Yeah ... maybe."

"Just ... don't push them away. You don't have to let them in," she tells me. "Not yet. But that doesn't mean you should push them away either."

I swallow hard, seeing the vulnerable look in her eyes. It's a quiet reminder that we've both pushed each other away before and neither instance went well for us. So, with a sigh, I tell her, "I'll think about it."

A smile tugs at her lips, and she presses a kiss to my jaw. "Good."

A few more minutes go by before I reluctantly climb out of bed, tugging Cecilia with me as we both get dressed. She squirms as she pulls on her underwear and jeans, and I quirk a brow, smirking as I watch her.

"So what should we—" The shrill of a phone pierces through the room. My eyes scan the room while Cecilia checks her pockets before we locate her phone on the floor a few feet away from the bed.

"Hello," she answers. "This is her." I watch her, half-naked and flushed, hair wild from me claiming her. She's a mess of contradictions—fragile yet strong, soft yet resilient. And she's all mine.

I head to my dresser for a pair of sweats, entirely naked and unashamed.

"Oh—" Something in her tone changes with that single word. I look over my shoulder as I shove my feet into my pants. Her skin pales, and her breath catches as she listens to whoever's on the other end of the line. The way her eyes lose focus, glassing over, tells me something's wrong.

Shit. And here I thought she might be checking me out the way I had been eyeing her.

I close the distance between us in three long strides, my hand on her hip as I tilt her chin up to meet my eyes. "What's going on?" I ask, voice low, but she shakes her head, stepping out of my grip, her body tense.

Fuck, I don't like this.

My fingers itch to take the phone from her and find out for myself what the hell is going on, but I know she won't like it. So, I wait.

She paces away from me, and I don't like that either.

My eyes track her as she walks around the room, stiff and agitated as she listens to the call. Every second feels like an eternity, and my patience is wearing thin. I want to know what's happening. I need to know.

Finally, she hangs up, turning to face me, her eyes wide and her lips trembling. "That was Mr. Ayala," she says, her voice shaking. "All three guys accepted their plea agreements. Sentencing is set for the week after next."

It takes a second for her words to sink in, for me to process what she's just said. Fuck. That's good, right? I mean, I think it's good. But judging by the freaked out expression on her face, I'm not so sure. I thought this was what she wanted.

"Are you okay with that?" I ask, my voice quieter than I expected.

She nods, her lips pressing into a thin line, and I can see some of the tension in her shoulders start to ease. "It's going to be over," she says. Cecilia's dark brown eyes shine with unshed tears and a hesitant smile curls the corners of her lips. "It's finally going to be over."

I pull her into my arms, my grip tight as I bury my face in her hair, breathing her in. "Yeah, baby. It's over."

twenty-one

CECILIA

I STEP INTO THE KITCHEN, my stomach growling softly as Gabriel follows close behind, his presence like a warm shadow.

"Hungry, baby?" he asks, his arms winding around my waist, pulling me against his chest. There's a smile in his voice, and I can't help but smile back, my lips tugging up even as I try to focus on the task at hand.

"A little," I admit, though my stomach's impatient grumbling says otherwise. "I have swim practice soon, but we've got time for a quick bite. Wanna eat with me before I go?" I glance back at him, catching his honey-brown eyes flicking down to my lips.

He tightens his hold, pressing a kiss to the side of my throat in that possessive way he does, making my knees feel weak. "I could eat." His voice is low, suggestive, and suddenly, this isn't just about food anymore.

How does he make something as simple as eating sound so dirty?

"What do you want?" I ask, slipping out of his hold and making my way toward the pantry, needing the small space to clear my head, to focus. Gabriel is a lot—intense, all-consuming, especially when his hands are on me. Not that I'm complaining.

He leans against the counter, watching me. "Whatever you want, baby. Surprise me."

I rummage through his pantry and pull out some ingredients. "How about pasta? Maybe a quick homemade marinara?"

One brow quirks up, amusement flickering in his eyes. "You can cook?"

I laugh, setting the cans of tomatoes and herbs on the counter. "Gabriel, I'm Italian. Cooking is literally in my blood."

Gabriel crosses his arms over his chest, a slow grin tugging at his lips as he watches me. His eyes stay locked on me, like he's trying to figure me out—always watching, always wanting. "You sure? Usually, I'm the one showing off in the kitchen."

"We'll see if you're still cocky after this." I roll my eyes playfully, grabbing a pot and filling it with water. "Watch and learn, Herrera. This is how we Italians do it." My hands move automatically, years of watching my mom and Nonna's hands at work making this second nature.

He steps closer, leaning in as I chop garlic and onions, tossing them into a pan with olive oil. The sizzle fills the air, followed quickly by the rich, fragrant aroma of garlic. Gabriel takes a deep breath, his eyes closing as he absorbs the smell. "Smells good already." I add in some fresh basil I found in the fridge. Shocker, I know. I didn't expect to find fresh basil in the fridge, either.

"You haven't seen anything yet," I tease, stirring the ingredients as the kitchen fills with the mouthwatering smell of a home-cooked meal. "This is how my nonna taught me—simple and fresh."

He watches me intently, his usual dominant energy muted, replaced with something softer, more curious. "I didn't know you had Italian roots."

"The dark hair, dark eyes, and soft tan didn't give it away?" I ask.

He shakes his head.

I grab a spoon to stir the sauce, letting the warmth of it settle the nervous energy building between us. "I'm Italian on both sides. Dad's mostly Italian with a sprinkle of Greek. Mom is half Italian, half Spanish," I explain. "Sundays were always pasta night at my house, and a good marina is one of the first things I learned how to make." I can feel him studying me, and it makes my heart race for reasons that have nothing to do with the cooking.

The sauce starts to bubble, the aroma growing richer. He reaches a finger toward the sauce, and I smack it away. "It's not ready," I admonish, ignoring his disgruntled frown.

Gabriel steals a piece of basil from the cutting board and pops it into his mouth with a triumphant, boyish smile. His nose wrinkles. "Delicious."

I laugh, knowing full well that raw basil tastes like black licorice. "Liar."

He grins and shrugs, stepping back just enough to grab two plates.

"So ... How's practice been?" I stir the sauce and lower the heat, letting it bubble gently as I glance over at him. It's hard to focus on anything but him, but I try to steer the conversation to safer ground. "You've seemed stressed lately." And I'd rather it be over soccer than because of me.

Gabriel exhales slowly, rubbing a hand through his hair. "It's been rough. Some of the younger guys ... they're good athletes, but we're not jelling. It's late in the season, and we still haven't found our rhythm. Everyone's in their own heads."

I nod, tasting the sauce and adding a pinch of salt. I can feel the tension in his voice, the frustration gnawing at him. "Maybe you guys need a break from the field. You know, something outside of soccer that helps you connect. One of those team building exercise things."

He tilts his head, considering the idea. "Like what?"

"I don't know. How about a team BBQ sometime before your next game?" I suggest, glancing over at him. "It could be a good way to get everyone on the same page. Build some chemistry."

"Yeah ... that's not a bad idea." He pauses, his gaze narrowing slightly as if another thought crosses his mind.

"And maybe ..." I check my pasta water and stall long enough to salt it. "You could invite Asher and Adam." The second the words leave my mouth, I see the change in his expression. The split-second shift from casual ease to strained tension. "I know you don't see them as family and I think that's fine," I rush to add before he has the chance to shut my idea down. "But, it can't hurt to get to know them better, right?"

Gabriel's jaw tightens, his easy going demeanor slipping for a moment. "I don't know ..."

"It was just an idea." I place a hand on his arm, squeezing gently. "I figured with the team there, you'd have a buffer. But, it's probably a bad idea, anyway. Forget I mentioned it."

He doesn't respond immediately, and I can see the internal battle playing out in his head. But finally, he lets out a sigh. "I'll think about it."

"Cool." I smile, reaching for the pasta. "Now, let's finish cooking so I can eat before I have to go."

The rest of the meal prep goes quickly, the tension easing between us as I throw the pasta into the boiling water, stirring it occasionally while the sauce continues to simmer. I can feel his eyes on me, that familiar warmth in his gaze, and it makes my heart skip a beat. There's something so intimate about cooking together, about sharing this simple piece of my heritage with him.

A few minutes later, I drain the pasta and mix it with the sauce, plating two bowls and sliding one over to him. Gabriel grabs two forks, handing me one as we sit down at the small kitchen table.

He takes a bite, closing his eyes briefly as he chews. "Damn, this is good."

"Better than your cooking?" I tease, twirling a forkful of pasta.

He chuckles, shaking his head. "Let's not get ahead of ourselves. Mexican food will always reign supreme."

We eat in comfortable silence, the tension from earlier melting away as we share the meal. Gabriel's mood seems lighter, more relaxed, and I'm glad we took this moment together. His leg brushes against mine beneath the table and butterflies dance in my stomach.

I don't know what it is. I just ... I really like being with him like this.

But as much as I wish I could stay, I glance at the clock, realizing I need to leave soon.

"I should head out," I say reluctantly after finishing my bowl, glancing at the clock. "Coach will kill me if I'm late for practice."

Gabriel stands, his expression softening. "I'll drop you off."

I shake my head, grabbing my phone. "It's okay. I already texted Adriana. She's going to swing by and pick me up on her way."

He doesn't argue, just watches as I gather my things. But before I can head to the door, he pulls me into his arms, his lips brushing against mine in a lingering kiss that leaves me breathless.

"You sure you don't want to stay?" he murmurs against my lips, his voice low and tempting. "You could skip practice. We could stay in. Have a movie night ..."

I laugh, swatting his chest playfully. "Nice try. I'll see you later."

He leans down, pressing one last kiss to my lips. "After practice." He doesn't voice it as a question but I answer him anyway.

"I'll try," I whisper, my heart so incredibly full as I head out his front door.

twenty-two

GABRIEL

THE COOL AIR brushes against my skin as I step out of the communications building, the bite of winter just around the corner, matching the chill creeping into my mood. I shift the weight of my bag on my shoulder. Everything feels a little heavier today, maybe because I miss having my girl here. Having Cecilia beside me in class, walking next to her through the crowded halls, the touch of her fingers brushing mine as we'd weave through campus like it was our own world.

Before all the shit with Austin, seeing her every weekday was a guarantee, part of my routine. But that's not the case anymore.

It's been four days since we shared a meal together at my place, and I hate how much I fucking miss her. We've both been running on empty—her dealing with attorney meetings about Austin's sentencing, a swim meet out of town, and me drowning in practices and classes. Even texting back and forth has been a struggle, and I hate it.

It's a stark contrast to when we'd grab lunch between classes, her exasperated smile always lightening my mood, no matter how shitty my day had been.

I run a hand through my hair, thinking about how it felt to kiss her goodbye the other day. She'd been heading out with Adriana, but the way her lips lingered against mine made it clear she missed me too. That connection between us, it's a lifeline I didn't know I needed until now.

As I cut across campus, my mind drifts to her, wondering what she's doing right now. Is she home studying or is she putting in some time in the pool?

Hell, I didn't even get to see her meet the other day. It sucks. I'm used to being there, cheering her on, supporting her. This whole week has just been … off.

My phone buzzes in my pocket, yanking me out of my thoughts. I pull it out and glance at the screen just as I spot Julio coming toward me, cutting through the parking lot.

His black hair is damp, clinging to his forehead, like he's just come from the locker room. I raise a hand in greeting, meeting him halfway.

"Yo, Gabe!" Julio calls, slapping my shoulder. "How was class?"

"Same as usual, man. What've you been up to?" I ask, wondering if I was supposed to train with him today and forgot.

Julio rubs the back of his tattooed neck. "Just putting in a little extra time in the gym," he tells me. "I had some free time and needed to work through some …" his expression twists into a scowl before he quickly masks it with a failed attempt at a casual shrug. "Just needed to work through some things."

Right. Some things. That look in his eyes—one I know too well

—tells me everything I need to know. "This wouldn't have anything to do with Adriana, would it?"

He huffs out a breath, his face tightening. "Of course not." But his answer comes too quick.

"Good." I try to keep my tone light. "I know she's been kicking it with that guy, Kenji. And I know you've—"

"Seriously, Gabe. I don't need to know. I couldn't care less who Adriana hangs out with or what she's up to."

His voice goes flat, and the tension rolling off him is almost visible.

"Right." It's obvious he doesn't want to talk about this though so I let the subject drop.

"Did you happen to see Coach while you were in the gym?" I ask, steering the conversation toward safer ground.

Julio's jaw tightens. "Yeah. He's still pretty pissed with how practices have been going."

"Fucking brutal. Coach ran us hard. Probably harder than we deserved, but I think he's pissed we're not clicking like we should be yet."

I pause, remembering Cecilia's suggestion the other day. "Cecilia had this idea. She mentioned we might need something to help us bond more. Like, maybe a team BBQ or something before the game this weekend. What do you think?"

Julio raises an eyebrow, mulling it over. He's silent for a beat, his eyes scanning the ground as he thinks. I can almost see the gears turning in his head, weighing the pros and cons. "Not a bad idea, actually. Could be exactly what we need to loosen everyone up. I'll talk to Coach, see if we can set something up."

"That'd be solid," I say, relieved he's on board. It's not like a BBQ is going to magically fix everything, but maybe some off-field bonding is what we need. Something's got to give. "We can keep it low-key, maybe grill at the soccer house." We don't usually invite people outside of our crew over, but I think in this instance, we can make an exception.

Julio nods, then tilts his head, his expression thoughtful. "Team-only thing, or do we let the guys bring a plus one?"

Fuck. My mind immediately goes to Asher and Adam. Shit. I'm not ready for that.

"What do you think?" I ask, deciding to take the decision out of my own hands. If J wants team only, then the decision is made. If he's cool with plus-ones ... nah. He's going to say team only. It's one thing to have them in our space. We might not all be best buds. But we at least know one another. No way is Julio going to be cool with literal strangers just—

"Let's do plus ones," he decides. "If we want the team to jell, they need to feel like we accept not only them but the people they care about."

That knot in my chest tightens. I swallow hard but manage a nod. "Yeah. Cool. I'll uh— I'll get with our boys and we'll grab groceries and shit this week while you figure out logistics and notify the team."

"Sounds good."

My phone buzzes again. Dad's name flashes across the screen, and my stomach dips.

"I'll catch you later," Julio says as I bring my phone to my ear.

"Yeah. Later," I mutter, watching Julio jog off before I answer the call.

"Hello?" I answer, still getting used to the fact that my dad actually calls me now. We've talked a little here and there since my mom's wedding but I'm still always taken off guard when he calls. Like it's some foreign and unexpected thing.

"Gabriel," his voice comes through, sounding tired but casual. "Just wanted to check in. How's everything going?"

"No complaints," I say, stepping out of the way of a group of freshmen headed for the dining hall. "Classes are classes. Soccer's been kicking my ass lately, though. The usual."

He chuckles, the sound short and quiet, but it's there. "Yeah, well, that's what you signed up for, isn't it?"

"Guess so," I reply, smirking at the sarcasm lacing his words.

"What about you? Work still crazy?" We tiptoe around the deeper shit. And we fully avoid topics that include Carlos or my mom. I haven't wholly forgiven my father, but I can't say I hate him anymore, either. Our relationship is complicated, but he's trying. And that's more than he's done before.

"It's always crazy," he answers, and I can practically hear him leaning back in his chair, probably rubbing the back of his neck like he does when he's stressed. "But I've been making time. I uh ... I went on a date last weekend."

I blink, not sure if I heard him right. Dad went on a date? Weird, but ... good, weird. Right? Mom went and found someone else already so I mean, why shouldn't he? "Yeah? How was it?"

"Good," he says, and I can hear his breath of relief through the phone. "We did dinner and a movie. Your old man's a little rusty, but I think it went well."

I laugh—because what else can I do? "Give it time, that rust will fall off real quick."

We chat a little longer, nothing deep, but casual and easy in a way that feels new between us. He asks me about the upcoming game. How things with Cecilia and me are going. He's trying, I realize. Really trying to make an effort, and for once, I don't feel like brushing him off.

"I'll see you at the game this weekend, right?" I ask, leaning against my bike. The matte black CBR 1000 rests under the sun like a shadow, its sleek lines swallowing the light. He's mentioned coming before, but I've learned not to expect much.

My pops hasn't been to a single game at PacNorth, and in high school, he barely made it to any of those. But hearing him say, "Wouldn't miss it," settles something inside me.

"Cool. I'll see you, then."

"Take care, Gabriel," he says.

"You too."

I hang up, staring at my phone for a second longer than necessary. That conversation wasn't earth-shattering, but ... it was good. It was something.

Throwing my leg over my bike, I rev the engine, the familiar rumble vibrating through me. As I pull out of the parking lot, my thoughts drift back to Asher and Adam, the BBQ, and what the hell it's going to be like having them there. But then I think about Dad, about how he's trying to patch things up.

Maybe Cecilia's right—maybe it's time I stop pushing people away.

twenty-three

CECILIA

CHLORINE CLINGS to the humid air as I step up to the edge of the pool. The familiar sound of splashing and laughter echoes off the walls—my team getting ready for practice. I pull my swim cap down over my hair, adjusting it as I glance around the room.

Willow flashes me a wave from across the pool. I wave back, smiling despite the brief flash of nerves. After that date with her brother Wyatt, I'd been half-expecting things to be awkward between us. I mean, it was fine, but no sparks. And then things got weird when Gabriel found out about it and they had their whole guy confrontation thing that she had a front row seat to. But, so far, she hasn't brought it up, and neither have I.

One less thing for me to worry about at least.

"Hey," Adriana's voice snaps me out of my thoughts, and I turn to see her beside me, a smirk tugging at her lips. "You ready to get your ass kicked today?"

...augh, tugging my goggles over my eyes. "It won't be that bad."

"Freestyle drills. All. Day," she groans dramatically, shaking her head like it's the worst thing in the world, but there's a glimmer of excitement in her dark eyes. Adriana thrives on the challenge.

I groan, but it's more out of habit than anything. The drills? I can handle them. Hell, I need them today. With everything going on—school, Gabriel, and my crazy schedule—swimming is the only place where I can shut my brain off and just *be*.

I was nervous about coming back here at first. I worried the pool would haunt me. That being here would bring all of the awful memories rushing back. But Austin Holt has taken enough from me. I refuse to let *him* steal this, too. Therapy helped with that, as much as I hate admitting it.

My therapist says trauma doesn't own spaces—we do. She's taught me how to take it back. To reclaim my peace. Maybe that's why I don't freak out anymore when unfamiliar men approach me. I don't like it, don't get me wrong. My heart still races. I still get that uncomfortable itch beneath my skin. But there's no longer this debilitating panic. No suffocating weight.

Coach Cho's sharp voice cuts through the noise, calling us to attention. "Alright, ladies! Show me clean strokes and focus on your form. No lazy arms today!"

Adriana rolls her eyes as we slip into the water, the cool rush instantly settling something inside of me. The world muffles as I submerge myself, leaving behind all the chaos of these past weeks.

The pool is one of the few places where everything else melts away—the noise, the stress, all the swirling thoughts about

Austin's sentencing. I just got word it's been scheduled for first thing Monday morning. One week away.

But right now, all I need to think about is me, the water, and the rhythm of my body cutting through it.

I push off the wall and focus on my breathing—two strokes, breathe, two strokes, breathe.

As we reach the wall, Adriana and I pop up at the same time, both panting slightly. "So," she says, already adjusting her cap for the next lap, "how's Gabriel?"

I smile, pushing my goggles up to my forehead. "Slammed with practice and training and everything," I sigh. "So busy, like me."

"That's what happens when you date a soccer player." She sticks her tongue out playfully, adjusting her goggles. "So unreliable."

I shoot her a pointed look, smirking. "Right. Because hockey players are so different?"

She grins. "Hockey players do appear to be the superior athletes."

"Oh really?" I say, "Do elaborate."

"What can I say," she tells me. "They answer when you call. They respond to your texts. They go out of their way to spend time with you. A girl like me could get used to it."

A laugh slips out of me. "Please tell me that is not where the bar's been set?"

"Definitely not. But you know what they say. Strong communication is the cornerstone for any good relationship."

chuckle, shaking my head. "So it's turning into a relationship, hmm? Sounds like Kenji might be a keeper."

She shrugs, trying to play it cool. "We'll see." But the soft curve of her lips gives her away.

"I'm happy for you," I tell her. "You deserve someone good in your life. And since I'm your best friend and therefore need to get to know any guy who might have an actual chance of sticking around, you should bring him with you when you come over for the barbeque at Gabriel's on Friday."

"Ladies! Get moving." Coach Cho's voice slices through our conversation.

"Shit." We adjust our goggles and dive back in. But when we pop back up at the other end, our conversation continues despite the fact that we're both breathless.

"Barbeque?" Adriana asks, "Those are usually family affairs. You know, just the guys." I don't miss the longing in her voice as she says it, and I remind myself she used to be a part of their friend group back in high school.

"They're doing a team thing," I tell her. "So there will be a lot of people there. I already cleared it with Gabriel the other day. He said you could come."

Her eyebrows shoot up, excitement flashing in her eyes before she frowns. "Really? He didn't seem put out by it?"

"Nope. He said I could invite whoever I want, so ... will you come? I don't know if any of the other players are bringing girlfriends, and I don't want to be the only girl there. Please."

She fidgets with her swim cap, chewing on the inside of her cheek—typical Adriana. Always in her head, overthinking

everything. "Okay, okay. I'll come. But if it's lame, I'm blaming you."

I splash her. "Fair enough."

"What would you do without me?" she jests.

"Probably drown and wallow in boredom," I confess.

"Mmm. So true," she says with a grin, finally letting go of her worry. She splashes me back before pushing off the wall again for another lap, and I race to catch up with her.

The water rushes past, muffling everything but the sound of my breath and the occasional splash of Adriana's strokes beside me.

As we finish our set, she treads water beside me and we wait for the rest of our team to wrap up their drills. "You seem excited about this BBQ," she notes, as we hoist ourselves onto the pool's ledge.

I shrug, trying to play it cool. "It's just ... I feel like I barely see him." I trail off, biting the inside of my cheek.

"Because of his practices?"

"Yeah, and swim, and coursework, and Austin crap," I say, my tone sharpening at the end. "It's like we're both just ... busy. And I don't know. I miss him, I guess."

"That's disgustingly adorable," she says, her gaze drifting to the pool deck for a moment. "You two don't get a lot of quality time, huh?"

"Not lately," I admit. "I can't wait for the semester to end, honestly. Online classes while living at home is driving me insane. I miss being on campus. I miss having an excuse to see him every day." God, I sound so needy.

riana stands up, her wet feet slapping against the pool deck as we retrieve our towels. "Ugh, I can't even imagine. I mean, I love my parents but living with them again," she shivers. "No thanks."

"Exactly." I grab my towel and wipe the water from my face. "I shouldn't have switched to online. And ... I think it's time I consider moving out, again."

"Really?"

I nod. "I need my own space. And my own routine, and ... normalcy. Maybe when all the Austin stuff is finally over," I sigh. I'm just so ready to have control over my own life again.

We walk toward the locker room, our teammates already heading in that direction, their laughter and chatter filling the space. Adriana slings her towel over her shoulder, eyeing me curiously.

"You thinking about the dorms again? Or are you looking off campus?"

"I don't know. I haven't really given it a lot of thought but—" I shrug. "I think it's time to."

Adriana's expression softens, and for a second, she looks like she's about to say something, but instead, she just pats my arm. "You still have time to figure it out."

"Yeah," I agree softly. "I guess I do."

"And hey, if you need to talk about any of the Austin stuff, you know I'm here, right?"

I nod, grateful for her offer even if I don't feel like diving into that mess right now. "Thanks. I appreciate it."

She smiles, nudging me with her shoulder as we push through the locker room doors. The scent of chlorine is even stronger in here, mixing with the smell of damp towels and soap.

"So," Adriana says as we step inside the locker room, her voice light again, "what are you going to wear to this BBQ? Please tell me you're going to rock something that'll make Gabriel lose his mind."

I laugh, shaking my head. "I'm thinking casual. It's not like I'm trying to seduce him in front of his teammates."

She rolls her eyes. "Please, if you showed up in sweats that boy would still be drooling all over you."

I snort, throwing my towel over the bench as I peel off my swimsuit. "Maybe. But I'll save the 'mind-blowing outfit' for after the BBQ."

She winks. "That's the spirit."

twenty-four

GABRIEL

"YO! HURRY THE HELL UP, MAN!" Felix hollers, wheeling the shopping cart down the aisle like he's training for a NASCAR pit stop. His energy radiates off him, buzzing, as if grocery shopping is a sport instead of a chore. He takes a sharp turn, barely missing an old lady by inches. My stomach drops.

"Felix!" I hiss, jogging over to the woman. Jesus. My heart races. "I'm so sorry," I say, my voice tight with embarrassment. "He's a little ... enthusiastic today."

She waves it off, her shaky smile attempting to reassure me. "Oh, no worries, dear. He gave me a little startle, that's all."

I nod, but the tension doesn't leave my shoulders until I'm halfway down the next aisle, trying to catch up to the idiot. "You're gonna run someone over, you dick," I mutter under my breath, yanking the cart to a halt. Felix is standing on the lower lip of the cart, coasting like a damn five-year-old. Sometimes I wonder how he makes it through his classes every day without adult supervision.

glances back, one eyebrow quirking. "We don't have all day, man. Meat's not gonna grill itself and people are going to start showing up to the house soon."

I roll my eyes. "If we get kicked out because you take out somebody's grandma, we won't have a BBQ at all. Also, I'd like to avoid a lawsuit, so just chill. Okay?"

Felix huffs, grabbing a random can off the shelf and holding it up. "Cheez Whiz. Great idea for an appetizer, yeah?" He smirks. There's that mischievous glint in his eyes that usually means trouble's about to follow.

I knew I should have made the store run solo.

"Put that shit back," I mutter, grabbing it from him and tossing it aside. We're here for carne, tortillas, and the essentials, not gross-ass Cheez Whiz. I steer us toward the meat counter, where the butcher gives us a once-over, probably wondering if we're serious customers or here to cause a scene.

"Seven pounds of Arrachera, please," I say, placing my order.

"Marinated or unmarinated?" he asks with a huff.

You can never trust American grocers to season their meat properly. A true arrachera is marinated with orange juice but these days, grocers have started using that artificial Sunny Delight shit. If they're going to use fake OJ, the least they can do is make it Tampico.

"Unmarinated," I tell him. The butcher weighs out the meat, making quick work of wrapping and packaging up our selection.

While we wait, Felix leans against the counter, his Aztec medallion swinging slightly as he rests his arms back against the clear glass. His grin stretches wide, and for a second, I get the feeling something's coming. Felix doesn't stay this quiet unless he's plotting something, and given the look on his face right now, it's something big.

I swear. He knows we have shit going on today. Now is not the time.

"Did Cecilia tell you Adriana's coming?" he asks, his tone casual. Too casual.

"Yeah." The meat thuds onto the counter, and I grab it, throwing it into the cart. "Why?"

Felix's smile grows even wider. "Did she tell you Adriana's bringing someone?"

My brows furrow. "No." But I don't see why that's an issue. She's probably bringing some chick from the swim team or something.

Is he waiting for me to freak out over that? If he is, he's going to be waiting a while.

Do I like strangers in my space? Not really. But Julio already decided we were allowing plus ones so what's one more stranger in my house? Honestly, Adriana's friend isn't going to make any difference.

"Interesting ..."

I stop mid-step, glancing over. Something coils tight in my gut, but I push it aside. "What's interesting?" I wait for him to elaborate, but when he doesn't, I sigh. "Out with it. Who's Adriana bringing?" He's getting too much pleasure out of dragging this out, and not only do we still have a lot of shit to do today, but frankly, I'm just not in the mood.

Felix clearly is in a great mood though because a grin practically splits his face in two as he says, "Adriana is bringing that hockey guy. Kenji."

A dull ache settles in the back of my skull. Kenji? "The dude we did that double date with?"

Felix nods, eyes bright with anticipation. "Yeah, him. She's bringing him to our house." He leans in, his voice dropping like he's revealing the world's biggest secret. "And not as a friend. He's coming as her date. Fuck—" he chuckles. "He might already be her boyfriend or some shit."

I blink, still not getting the big deal. "Okay?" I shrug, tossing a few packs of tortillas into the cart. "What's the problem? He's decent. Not some frat douche." He could have picked a better sport because really, hockey? But I mean, we all make mistakes in life.

Felix groans, planting his face in his hands. "Dude, you can't be this dense. This isn't just about him. It's about Adriana bringing a date. To our place. The place where we," he indicates the space between us, "live with three other guys. Any guesses over which one will take issue with Adriana bringing a date into his home?"

I stop short, the realization hitting me square in the face.

Shit.

Julio.

"Oh fuck."

"Yeah. Fuck is right." Felix says, voice almost gleeful now. "Shit's gonna blow up today, and I don't know about you, but I'm ready to see some fireworks. This is like four or five years in the making."

My mind churns with all the possible ways Julio might handle Adriana walking in with a date. None of them are good. Despite what Julio says, he has a thing for her. Always has, ever since we were kids. But he never seemed interested in crossing that line with her.

There was that one time he drunkenly made out with her at a party but according to Julio, it was a mistake and he didn't realize who he was kissing in the moment. None of us really bought his story back then, but it wasn't worth getting into. But now —

"Did you give J a heads up at least?" I push the cart toward the checkout, my chest tight.

Felix grins. "Where would the fun be in that?"

"Come on," I tell him. "You've got to give the guy a warning."

"Pass," Felix says. "I've been starving for entertainment and I'm telling you, man, this BBQ is about to get real interesting." He rubs his hands together. "I can hardly wait."

I grimace. The last thing we need is drama, especially with the team coming over. "We can't have him blowing up at the BBQ."

Felix laughs, already grabbing the bags from the checkout. "Oh, yes. We can. It's gonna be great. Like a fucking telenovela." He's already heading toward the door, excitement buzzing in his steps.

I jog to catch up, my mind tangled in thought. Julio, Adriana, Kenji. Maybe if we can keep them in separate parts of the house ... If I can reduce the risk of them crossing paths ...

We load the groceries into the truck and head straight back home. I get why Felix was in a hurry to return because I'm eager to get back to the house as well, though for entirely different reasons. Felix doesn't want to miss the show. And I ... I need to make sure one never starts.

As soon as we pull into the driveway, my eyes land on Cecilia's white Jeep and an unfamiliar Ford Bronco parked in front of the house. That knot in my stomach twists tighter. I spot Julio through the large front window, arms folded, jaw clenched tight as he glowers at the world outside.

"Told you, man." Felix lets out a low whistle. "Shit is about to go down."

I stop dead, watching Julio, who's staring at the Bronco like it personally insulted him. Shit. This is gonna get ugly.

Felix grins, practically skipping to the door. "Man, I give it fifteen minutes before Julio blows a gasket. This is gonna be epic."

I shake my head, unease gnawing in my gut. "Epic or a disaster," I mutter, following Felix up the steps.

My mind's already working on damage control.

twenty-five

GABRIEL

I STEP into the soccer house, tension pulling at my shoulders. I'm not sure what I'm walking into, but from the looks of it, Julio is waiting for me. If I know him at all, he's already fuming about Adriana bringing Kenji. I honestly don't know how I overlooked that. The guy's denied anything going on between them for years but fuck—we all know there's something. He made that pretty obvious with how pissed he was when he found out about the double date in the first place.

The air inside feels heavier than usual, thick with anticipation, like it's charged and just waiting for the spark to ignite. My fingers tighten around the grocery bags as I scan the room, searching for the first sign of trouble.

But instead, my eyes latch onto her.

Cecilia stands by the staircase, wearing one of my hoodies, her smile hitting me like a shot of pure sunlight. Her eyes light up the moment they meet mine. I don't even pause to think. I just react. Everyone and everything else in the room fades for a second. The bags of groceries I'm holding drop to the floor with a thud, and I close the distance between us in two long strides, sweeping her up into my arms.

She giggles, her legs latching around my waist as I lift her feet off the ground. Her laugh melts away the weight on my shoulders, and I tighten my grip on her thighs, pulling her closer. Cecilia wraps her arms around my neck, her body warm and familiar against mine.

"Missed you," I murmur, pressing my nose into the curve of her neck. The sweet, familiar scent of her coconut shampoo fills my senses. Fuck she smells good.

"I missed you, too," she whispers back, her breath warm against my skin. I hold her there for a moment longer, just breathing her in. The noise of the others talking dulls to a background hum, and I find myself just wanting to stay in the moment.

When I finally set Cecilia back on her feet, I lean forward and capture her mouth in a kiss. I mean for it to be quick, just a taste, but the second her lips meet mine, I'm gone. Her lips are soft. Her mouth so inviting. She tastes like cherry cola—sweet and fizzy, and before I can stop myself, I deepen the kiss, pulling her closer.

It's not enough. It never is. This desire between us bordering on desperation. I really wish we weren't about to have a house full of people right now.

A throat clears, and I pull back, blinking away the haze of Cecilia's lips. I glance up to find Adriana standing nearby, Kenji right next to her. Adriana raises an eyebrow, amusement stamped across her features while Kenji offers a small wave.

"Sorry to interrupt," Adriana says, though it's obvious she isn't. There's a hint of something guarded in her smirk but if I had to guess, it has nothing to do with our impromptu PDA and everything to do with the read she has on Julio's mood.

Kenji, on the other hand, looks relaxed. His hands are shoved into his pockets as he watches us with a smile on his face. The guy doesn't look like he has a care in the world. I almost envy him.

I force myself to release my girl, nodding to Kenji. "Hey, man."

Cecilia steps out of my arms, her delicate fingers slipping into mine, and I turn my attention to the real problem—Julio. He's across the room, his jaw tight, nostrils flaring as he watches Kenji like he's some kind of intruder. The tension is rolling off him in waves, heavy and hot.

I already know today is going to be a long day.

"Have you met everyone yet?" I ask.

"He hasn't," Adriana answers for him. "Some people have been too busy brooding to introduce themselves."

I wince. Did she really just call J out like that? Adriana isn't dumb—she knows exactly what she's doing. But provoking Julio? Not the best idea.

"Julio, this is Kenji," I say, keeping my tone casual, like introducing these two isn't a recipe for disaster. "Kenji, this is Julio."

Julio's jaw clenches tighter, the muscle ticking in his cheek. His dark eyes narrow, but he grunts in acknowledgment. "Sup." The word is clipped, cold. He's not even trying to be friendly, not even a little.

Kenji, to his credit, doesn't seem fazed. "Nice to meet you," he says, sticking out his hand. "You're the Captain, right?" Julio takes a beat too long to respond, but finally, he shakes Kenji's hand—a little too firm, too aggressive. Typical.

"Yup," Julio mutters, his expression unreadable. At least he bothered to respond.

Kenji's smile doesn't falter. "Sick, man. I've heard a lot about you." The admiration in his voice seems genuine, but Julio's expression doesn't budge.

Before Julio can make shit any more uncomfortable, Felix bounds over, throwing an arm around my shoulders. "You gonna introduce me too?" he asks. Felix never fails to lighten the mood, even when shit's about to hit the fan.

"Kenji, Felix," I say, grateful for the interruption. "Felix, Kenji. There. You've been introduced."

Felix grins wide, his gold chain catching the light. "Ah, you're the hockey guy, right?" At Kenji's nod he adds, "Don't worry. We won't hold that against you. For today at least."

Kenji laughs, shaking Felix's hand. "Thanks, man. Appreciate it."

We make quick introductions to the rest of the guys, Atticus and Deacon trailing down from upstairs to join the group. The tension in Julio's posture is impossible to ignore, but I do my best, focusing instead on keeping things moving.

"Felix and I grabbed the meat," I say, pointing to the bags I'd unceremoniously dropped earlier. "J, why don't you get the grill going?"

Julio's eyes flick toward the bags, then back to me. For a second I think he might push back, but then he jerks his chin in a nod, turning toward the kitchen to get things prepared. At least cooking will give him something to focus on other than glaring daggers at Adriana's date all day.

The doorbell rings, saving us from any more awkwardness, and my teammates start pouring in.

The tension eases as the house fills, the smell of grilling meat wafting in from the backyard. I grab a beer, crack it open, and take a long pull. Things are settling down. *Good.*

"You good?" Cecilia asks.

I nod and press a kiss to her temple. "I'm perfect," I tell her. "You're here."

She smiles up at me, and I resist the urge to kiss her, barely. When the doorbell rings again. Layton—a junior who plays center back—opens the door and Adam and Asher walk in.

The sight of them pulls me up short. They're here, standing in my house, and it feels ... strange. Not bad, exactly, but not comfortable either.

My new stepbrothers are greeted by Layton and Atticus at the door before they spot Kenji and make a beeline straight for him. I exhale a breath of relief watching as Asher claps Kenji on the back like they've known him for years. I guess they kind of have, considering they all play hockey together.

I watch them for a second, the way they laugh and joke like it's nothing. Like being here, in my home, isn't at all a problem for them. A knot tightens in my chest. I wish I could explain how them being here makes me feel. I see Asher shove his brother's shoulder jokingly and then Adam elbows him back. It's playful and fuck—I don't know. I think ... I think I miss that.

"You invited them?" Cecilia says beside me, her tone cautious.

I grunt, taking another pull from my beer. I'm not much of a drinker, but today? I'll make an exception.

Cecilia winds her arms around my waist, her warmth seeping through the thin material of my shirt. "I'm glad," she says. "They seem nice."

"Maybe," I hedge, my eyes flicking back to them. "I'm going to make my rounds, say hello to the guys. You want to come with me?"

"Nah," she tells me. "You go do your thing. I have Adriana."

I steal one last kiss before heading toward the grill, where Julio's flipping the carne asada with an intensity that borders on murderous. I offer him a beer, which he takes with a grateful nod, but his scowl doesn't budge.

"Didn't think you'd go through with it," Julio mutters, his eyes flicking in the direction of Adam and Asher.

I shrug, taking a long swig from my bottle. "Yeah, well. Maybe I'm growing up."

Julio huffs a laugh, shaking his head. "Proud of you, man. Letting them in, giving them a shot. That's a big deal."

I shoot him a sideways glance. "Maybe you should take your own advice," I tell him, tapping my bottle against his. "You know, give Kenji a shot. He's not that bad, and Adriana seems to like him."

Julio grumbles something under his breath, flipping the meat with more force than necessary, and I roll my eyes. It's the closest thing to agreement I'm gonna get from him today.

After a few minutes, I spot Asher making his way over to me. He looks a little awkward, like he's not sure if he's intruding, but I lift my chin, signaling him over. May as well get this part of the day over with.

"Hey," Asher says, his voice casual, but there's a cautious thread beneath his carefree demeanor. "Thanks for the invite."

"Yeah. No problem."

We stand there for a beat, the sounds of chatter and sizzling meat filling the silence between us. "I know—" His mouth twists and he tries again. "I get that this is probably weird for you," Asher begins, rubbing the back of his neck. "It's a little weird for me, too."

I take a slow pull from my beer, studying him. "It's fine."

He nods, but his expression is unconvinced. "Adam was really excited when we got your text. It meant a lot to him. You reaching out like that. So, I guess I, uh ..." He stares down at his feet for a moment. "I just wanted to thank you. You didn't have to reach out but ... I'm glad you did."

I glance across the yard where Adam's laughing with Kenji, and something shifts in my chest. I get it. Asher cares about his brother the way I cared about mine.

"You look after him."

Asher nods. "Yeah. I mean, he's my baby brother. Wouldn't you if you were in my shoes?" He winces as soon as the question leaves his mouth. "I didn't—"

"It's fine," I tell him. "Really."

Silence stretches between us again.

"Sorry. I just," Asher lifts his chin to the sky, searching for his words. "I know this can't be easy for you. It's weird as fuck for me."

"Yeah," I mutter, glancing back at Julio, who's still glaring daggers in Kenji's direction. "It's weird as fuck for me too."

He chuckles. "Well, that's something at least."

I match his grin and some of the tension between my shoulders dissipates. We stay like that for a while, each of us drinking our beers and watching the rest of the partygoers around us.

"He's a good kid," Asher tells me. When I give him a confused look, he clarifies, "Adam. He's a good kid. He follows the rules. Never gets into trouble. That kid lives and breathes hockey, and he's really talented. He sketches and is like, artistic and shit."

I nod along to what he says, not really sure why he's bothering to tell me any of this.

"Okay."

"I just ... he's a good kid."

"So you've said."

Asher curses under his breath. "Sorry. Fuck." He shakes his head, his mouth grimacing. "Look, can I be honest with you for a minute?"

Julio's eyes lock with mine over Asher's shoulder. He raises a brow in a silent question as if to ask, *what is this guy's deal?*

I shake my head and return my attention to Asher because fuck if I know. Julio shrugs, turns off the grill, and piles a plate high with meat before taking it over to the outside tables where most of our team seem to have set up camp.

"Shoot," I tell him.

Asher spends a few seconds glancing around and collecting his thoughts. "Adam really wants you to like him," he says.

"Alright." I mean, I can't make any promises. I barely know the guy. But I invited them, didn't I? I'm not trying to be a dick. I'd like to think I'm giving the kid a fair shake.

"He has this idea in his head," Asher tells him. "Like the three of us can be real brothers. Or at the very least ... I don't know. Best fucking friends or something like that."

I snort. I don't mean to. It just sorta slips out.

"The guy doesn't even know me," I say.

"I know. But Adam is ... he's different. He gets attached to people easily and since your mom married our dad he just ...," he grimaces. "He's going to push his way into your life. Or at least, he's going to try."

"Why?" I ask. He's got his brother. From the look of things, at least one parent that he likes. I don't know what the deal is with their mom but they were groomsmen in their dad's wedding so there's got to be some sort of decent relationship there.

"Because family is the single most important thing to him," Asher tells me. "And as far as Adam is concerned, you're a part of ours."

"Good for him," I tell him. "But I already have a family." I tip my beer toward Julio before pointing at the rest of my roommates and ending with Cecilia. "The one I was born into didn't work out so I built my own."

Asher nods, his expression contemplative. "I get that," he says. "But I'm asking you to give my brother a chance. You don't have to accept or even like me. I'm cool with where we currently stand. But Adam is sensitive. Just … tell me what it is that you need from me to give my brother a chance?"

My jaw clenches. I don't like the position he's putting me in right now. I'm not trying to be a dick but he's not asking for any small favor. Allowing them into my life, into my family, that's a risk I'm not sure I'm willing to take.

"Why me?" I ask. "He's got a new mom he can go connect with. Why not focus his energy there?"

"No offense man, but your mom is—"

"A piece of work." I finish for him.

He huffs out a breath. "Yeah. I mean, my dad loves her so I guess there's that. She's just …" His lips press together and his brows pull forward as he mulls over whatever it is he was about to say.

"She's selfish," I tell him. "She might act like she loves your father and maybe she really does. But she does so because he offers her something of value. Money, or security, or maybe just the feeling of being wanted. I don't really know. My mom has her own baggage I'm not willing to try and unpack. But her love comes with conditions. I'm assuming you've already realized this?"

"Yeah. It was fine at first. I mean she's nice and all but it's like nothing we do is good enough. She nitpicks the stupidest things and sometimes it feels like she's trying to turn us into people that we're not."

I don't bother telling him she's recreating the family she lost. He'll figure it out eventually.

"I don't know what to tell you, man. She is who she is. I stopped trying to figure out her motives years ago."

Asher sighs. "I get it," he tells me. "But Adam was really looking forward to the whole big happy family thing, and since he's not going to find that with your mom ... "

"He's turned his attention to me?"

He shrugs. "Yeah. I guess you could say that."

My fingers tighten around the bottle in my hand. "I'm not looking to replace my dead brother," I tell him.

Asher's shoulders slump, and his expression falls with defeat. "Right. Yeah. Um."

"But I'm open to considering friends."

His head jerks up, dark brown widening. "Yeah?"

I nod. "Yeah. We can start with friends."

twenty-six
CECILIA

THE BARBEQUE LOOKS to be a hit. Some of Gabriel's teammates toss a football around the yard, while others sit at the outdoor tables eating food and relaxing. I move through the crowd, my eyes scanning the open space when I catch a glimpse of Kenji laughing with a few of the guys.

"He seems to be fitting in," I tell Adriana.

"Mmm ..." She makes a noncommittal sound before taking a drink of her beer. I shudder just thinking about the taste. I haven't touched a drop of alcohol since the party with Austin last summer. And despite knowing that I'm safe—that Gabriel would never let anything like that happen here—I'm not sure I ever will.

What went down that night wasn't the result of alcohol. I know that, so my aversion to it seems a bit silly. But drinking feels like a slippery slope, and despite the progress I've made, I'm not sure I'm capable of letting loose like that. Not with this many people around. With so many unknowns.

Even now there's an itch beneath my skin. This sense of urgency that I need to leave. To find somewhere safe. But I know it's just the fear. I haven't had a panic attack in weeks and I'm not about to have one today.

"You doing okay?" Adriana asks, her head tilted to the side as she looks me over.

"Yeah. Of course." My voice is a little too breathless. A little too high.

"Julio still doesn't look happy, though," I tell her, hoping to divert her attention. Her head twists in his direction, and her lips press into a thin line.

"He's such a child," she snaps, nostrils flaring. "And I swear to god, if he doesn't stop acting like such a prick, I'm going to give him a piece of my mind."

"Maybe you should." As soon as the words come out of my mouth, I immediately regret them, but it's too late to take them back.

Adriana's eyes brighten, a determined look washing over her face. "You know what?" she says, "You're right. I should."

"No, no. I—"

"I'll be back," she tells me. "I'm going to tell this cabrón it's time he pulls that stick out of his ass."

"Adriana, wait!" But she's already stomping across the yard and I'm sorry, I don't have a death wish. I'm sure Julio can take care of himself because no way am I going to be foolish enough to go and follow her. That man is on his own.

My eyes flick toward the far side of the yard where Gabriel stands with Asher, the older of his two new stepbrothers. I watch them for a moment, worry crawling up my spine. Gabriel's back is straight, his shoulders tight and even from this distance, I know he's uncomfortable.

Asher says something, and for a second, Gabriel's mouth quirks into a smile, but it's fleeting. After another minute or two, Asher walks off, heading back over to his brother, Adam, as Gabriel watches him go.

His hand tightens around the neck of his beer as he pulls the bottle to his lips and takes a slow drink.

I make my way over to him, the knot in my chest pulling tighter. "Hey," I call softly. "How's it going?"

He glances at me as I approach, his expression unreadable for a moment before he shrugs. "Fine."

I raise an eyebrow. "Fine?"

His lips pull into a tight smile, but it doesn't reach his eyes. "All good, baby."

I study him for a beat longer, considering whether or not to pry. I'm curious to know how his talk went with Asher. But it's obvious Gabriel doesn't want to talk. Not when we're surrounded by people at least.

Instead, I nudge his arm lightly, offering a small smile. "Good. I'm glad everything is going smoothly. The guys seem to be having a good time."

"Yeah." Gabriel draws me into his side, and I sink into his embrace. "This was a good call," he says. "Thank you." He presses his lips to my temple, and I exhale a breath of relief. But just as I allow myself to relax, Adriana's voice slices through the air like a whip, sharp and cutting.

"You are such an asshole!"

Her words ring out, turning heads like an arrow ripping through silence. I turn in time to see Adriana standing in front of Julio, her face flushed with anger, her eyes blazing. She's gripping Kenji's hand so tightly her knuckles are white, and every muscle in her body looks ready to snap.

The world around us seems to freeze. The casual conversations stop, the laughter dies, and every single person in the yard stares.

Julio doesn't shout back. He doesn't even move. He just stands there, jaw clenched, nostrils flaring, his hands at his sides like he's barely holding it together. And then something flickers across his face, something that surprises me—disappointment. It's not the reaction I was expecting. I was waiting for the explosion. For the anger to erupt, but instead, there's just ... defeat.

His chin dips and with a shake of his head, he turns his back and heads through the glass slider and back into the house.

Without another word, Adriana pulls Kenji with her, storming toward the gate, her back rigid as she practically drags him out. I watch them go, my heart sinking into my stomach. Whatever just happened, it wasn't good.

I glance back at Gabriel, who's staring at Julio, his jaw tight, but his expression torn. He doesn't know what to do either.

"I should go check on her," I say, my voice quieter now. "Make sure she's okay."

Gabriel's eyes never leave Julio, who's staring at the floor now, his shoulders sagging like the weight of whatever just went down is crushing him. He nods, but there's a heaviness in his

238

gesture. "Yeah ... maybe it's a good idea. I'll go in too and check on J."

We slip through the house, the buzz of conversations rising again as the yard returns to some semblance of normal, but the tension follows us, wrapping around my chest like a vice. Things are weird between the two of them, and I had no business getting involved in any of it. I wish I'd just kept my mouth shut.

We move through the living room and kitchen, past people who have no idea what just happened outside. I half expect Adriana to be fuming somewhere out front, trying to calm down, but as I reach the front door, it's obvious she's not here. She actually left.

I pull out my phone, typing a quick text with shaky fingers.

> **Me:** Are you okay? What happened?

My phone buzzes a second later, and I glance down.

> **Adriana:** I'm fine. Julio is a dick and you can tell him to go fuck himself.

Yeah, so, I won't be doing that.

> **Me:** Do you need to talk? I can meet you at your place if you want.

I frown as I reread my own text. I don't really want to leave. I was looking forward to spending some time with Gabriel but if Adriana needs me, I'll be there. Quality time will just have to wait.

> **Adriana:** That's ok. Kenji's with me. We're going to do our own thing. I'll talk to you later.

"She good?" Gabriel asks, peering over my shoulder.

"She says she's fine," I tell him. "They're just gonna go hang out on their own."

Gabriel nods, but I can see the tightness in his expression. Whatever happened with Adriana and Julio isn't fine and it's not okay. Julio looked ... wrecked.

"Well," Gabriel's voice is softer now, edged with something that pulls at the corners of his mouth, "since we're inside, and things seem to be going fine out there ..." He steps closer, his hand slipping around my waist, his lips grazing my ear. "Maybe we could sneak upstairs. Get some alone time. Just the two of us."

I blink, half-smiling despite myself. "Are you serious right now?"

His grin is pure mischief. "Completely."

I shake my head, laughing under my breath. "Gabriel, you're hosting a barbeque for your team. It's supposed to be a bonding experience. You can't just abandon them to sneak off and screw—"

"Who said anything about sneaking off to have sex?" His eyes widen with exaggerated innocence. "Maybe I just want to cuddle. Talk about our feelings."

"Uh-huh." I roll my eyes, but I'm fighting a smile. "Sure. Because you're the picture of wholesome intentions, right?"

"Damn straight." He steps closer, pressing his forehead to mine, his voice dropping to a low murmur. "I'm a pure, innocent man."

"Right." I laugh softly. "Pure as sin."

Gabriel's grin widens as he leans in. His lips brushing against my ear, sending shivers down my spine. "You know you want to go upstairs with me. Nobody has to know we snuck off for a quicky," he tells me. "It's okay every now and then to be a little bad."

His words send heat rushing to my cheeks, and I swallow the urge to melt against him. He's good at this. Too good.

"You," I say, pulling back just enough to meet his eyes, "are staying here and being a good host. No sneaking off. Besides, weren't you going to go check on Julio?"

"Fine." He sighs, dramatically, like I've just broken his heart. "But you owe me for this."

I laugh, grabbing his hand and steering him toward the staircase that leads to not only Gabriel's but also Julio's bedroom. "Go check on your friend. And then get your butt back outside before your teammates think their Captain and Striker have ditched them."

"I'm going. I'm going."

twenty-seven

GABRIEL

FOR ALL INTENTS AND PURPOSES, the barbeque yesterday was a success. Julio never came back out after his beef with Adriana, and being the insufferable fucker he is, he refused to talk about what happened. I'm going to remember that the next time he pushes and pries his way into my shit. But despite his disappearing act, the rest of the guys seemed to enjoy themselves. Everyone ate and drank and had a good time. Asher and Adam stayed for most of the day, and as much as it pains me to admit this, they're pretty decent guys. The kind who, under normal circumstances, I wouldn't mind watching a game or sharing a meal with.

I don't know how much of a relationship I'm willing to have with either of them but we agreed to meet up and train together once a week. They have to put time in the gym for hockey just like I do for soccer so it's an easy enough way to get to know them. I'll drag one of my roommates with me in the beginning at least.

"Yo," Julio calls out, his voice booming through the crowded locker room. "Everyone ready?"

The guys all cheer, fists pumping into the air. Lockers are slammed closed and everyone makes whatever last minute adjustments they need to before we head out onto the field while Coach comes forward to begin his, *we've got this,* speech.

"He's better today." Felix nudges me with his elbow, keeping his voice low so as not to draw any attention. "You think his head's in the game?"

I give a slight shake of my head. "No." And that's a problem. "You saw him last night. He spent all evening moping around after everyone left, constantly checking his phone like he couldn't decide whether or not to message her."

"He needs to get his head in the game," Felix mutters.

Even now when we're about to step out onto the field, Julio is discreetly glancing at his phone screen for what I know is at least the hundredth time today.

"Does he think she's going to call him?" Felix asks.

"Hope he's not holding his breath."

Adriana is stubborn. Fiercely independent. And I can count on one hand the number of times that girl has ever tucked tail or apologized.

I've got Julio's back. No matter what. He's family. But shit between him and Adriana is complicated, and from where I'm standing, he's the one who was being a dick all afternoon yesterday. The two of them need to just sit down and hash out their shit. Especially since Adriana and Cecilia are friends now. She's going to be around more. There's no avoiding that. And for all our sakes, they need to find a way to get along.

Julio doesn't like that she's got a new man in her life and I get it. If I were in his shoes, I probably wouldn't be happy about their situation either. But if he doesn't want Adriana seeing somebody else, then he needs to put his cards on the table and finally admit to how he feels about her.

Until he grows a pair and does that, she's going to continue living her life.

You can't blame her for it.

"—so get out there and show the Devils what PacNorth Wolves are made of!" Coach finishes his speech and everyone shouts out a variation of "Hell yeah," and "we've got this," slamming their fists against the doors of their lockers and rallying together as a team.

"Come on," I tell Felix, falling into step beside Atticus and Deacon. "We've got a game to win."

———

THE WHISTLE BLOWS, AND ELEVEN OF US TAKE THE FIELD, our cleats pounding against the turf.

The crowd roars, cheering for us as we get into position. My heart races, adrenaline thrumming through my veins. This is what we've been training for. All those practices, the endless fucking drills, it's all for this.

I'm locked in, every muscle coiled and ready. But when I glance over at Julio, I can already tell—he isn't focused. He's staring off toward the sideline, his shoulders tense, and I know exactly what's caught his eye.

Adriana.

She's sitting in the second row, my girl on her left and you know who on her right. Fuck. I don't give a shit who she dates but we're going to have to lay down some ground rules when it comes to our games. I can't have my boy's head messed up like this.

I clench my jaw, focusing back on the game. I need him switched on. To focus on what really matters right now. We all do. Julio's our captain, our anchor. But right now? He's fucking distracted, and it's going to turn him into a liability during the game.

Deacon slides up next to me, bumping my shoulder with his. "You seeing this?"

"Yeah. I'm seeing it."

Julio hasn't barked orders at anyone. Hasn't fired us up with his usual cocky-ass swagger. It's like he's somewhere else entirely. And on a day like today, with the league's top team staring us down, that's a problem we can't afford.

"Think he'll snap out of it?" Deacon asks, eyes locked on the ball as Atticus lobs it upfield.

I shake my head, tracking the play. "Doubt it. Not today."

The ball moves fast, and I take off, sprinting past the defenders. For a second, everything else fades—the noise, the tension, my frustration with Julio—it's just me and the pitch, my legs pumping, adrenaline surging.

I weave around a defender, spot the gap, and make the run. Deacon sends it to me with a quick pass, and I drive the ball up the field. I have two defenders on me so I kick it up to one of our forwards—Rion Pru. He swings his leg back and fires off the shot.

The ball sails just wide of the goal, missing the net by inches.

"Fuck!" I slam my hand against my thigh, frustrated with the miss, but not letting it slow us down.

"Shit. I'm—" Rion stammers.

"Don't worry about it," I tell him. "We've got time. This is only the start of the game."

"Shake it off!" Deacon shouts, already moving back into position.

I throw him a nod and we all hustle to reset, but it's hard not to notice Julio dragging behind. His pace is slower, his eyes still drawn somewhere else. And when the opposing team makes a break, I watch in disbelief as he lets their midfielder slip right by him without any kind of a challenge.

"Julio! What the fuck, man?" I snap, charging toward the guy with the ball, trying to clean up his mess. I manage to shoulder the guy off balance, stealing the ball back. I shoot a glare at Julio as I pass him. He doesn't even look at me.

"What the hell was that?" Deacon mutters as he pulls alongside me, his long legs easily keeping pace. "It's like he zoned out."

"No shit." My chest tightens with frustration.

The game continues, but it's more of the same. Julio's distracted, always a step behind, and every time I glance his way, he's got his eyes on the stands—his attention trained on Adriana and Kenji. "Come on, man!" I shout. "Get your head in the game!"

Then it happens—Julio mistimes a challenge, his footwork sloppy. The other team's striker doesn't hesitate, sidestepping him with ease, leaving Julio behind like he's not even there. It's a straight path to Atticus and our goal net.

I sprint, trying to close the distance, but I'm too far back.

Atticus dives, but the ball skims past his gloves and sinks into the back of the net.

0-1. Just like that.

Julio stands there, staring at the ground, his hands on his hips. His face is twisted in disbelief. Like he doesn't understand how Suncrest U managed a goal. *Newsflash cabrón, you let it through.*

"Goddammit, Julio!" I shout as we regroup. I don't have time to babysit his feelings right now.

Felix jogs over, wiping the sweat off his brow. "Man, we can't keep playing like this."

"We won't," I growl, pacing, trying to shake off my own irritation. "If he doesn't snap out of it, I'm going to lose my shit."

Coach calls for a water break, and I use the opportunity to stalk over to Julio. He's off to the side, rubbing the back of his brightly colored tattooed neck. I can see him trying to get back in the zone, but whatever it is he's telling himself, it isn't having the desired effect.

I step into his space, not caring if he's in the mood to talk or not. "You need to get your head in the game, man. Right now. This isn't just about you. We lose this one and we lose the NCAA committee pick."

He finally looks at me, his face tight. "I know, alright? I fucking know."

248

"Do you? Because it sure as hell doesn't look like it. You're letting her mess with your head, and it's fucking us up out here."

Julio's jaw clenches, his nostrils flaring. For a second, I think he might take a swing at me, but he doesn't. He just exhales sharply, his eyes narrowing. "It's not that simple."

"It is that simple. You're our captain. On this field, that's all that matters. Be that guy and help your team win the game. You can be your usual broody fucking self when you walk off this field, but until then, she doesn't exist. Understand?"

He doesn't say anything. Just stares at the ground like it's got all the answers.

"Look, man," I say, softening my tone a little. "You've got to deal with your shit, but not right now. Not when we've got a game to win."

Julio's gaze flicks back to the field, and something clicks in his eyes. I don't know if it's enough, but it's something.

He gives a curt nod. "Yeah. Alright."

We head back out, and I can see him trying, putting in more effort, but it's not the Julio we're used to. The fire's not there, not the way it should be. And we're down because of it. Our team was already struggling. The barbeque was supposed to bring us all together. Help us get into sync.

Not tear our captain apart.

The rest of the game is a grind. We manage to score four goals during the first half but Suncrest U makes nine, and in the second, we just can't close the fucking gap. When the final whistle blows, we finish with a score of 5-12.

Disappointment hits like a punch to the gut.

I shake hands with the other team, but my mind's already checked out.

Back in the locker room, I glance at Julio. He's sitting on the bench, staring down at his phone. *More of this shit?* He hasn't said a word to any one of us since the game ended.

I grab a towel, wiping the sweat off my face. I want to say something, but what's the point?

Jameia steps into the locker room with her hand over her eyes. "Everybody dressed?" she calls out.

A chorus of "Yes," greets her.

She lowers her hand, a somber smile tugging at her lips as her dark brown eyes sweep across the room. She wore her box braids up today, twisting them into a complicated knot atop her head. She makes her way over to Julio, who's slouched and shirtless on the bench like he's got the weight of the world on his shoulders.

His body is a canvas of ink, giving our assistant coach her first look at his heavily decorated skin. Jameia's eyes take each of his designs in, and I watch her gaze travel from the lotería cards that climb down and around his neck to the intricate Aztec necklace that stretches across his collarbone and the top of his chest.

The centerpiece is a stylized eagle head encircled in geometric patterns and Aztec glyphs, forming an almost armor-like shape across his chest. That piece took fifty-five hours to complete, and I was with him for every single one of them.

But J's ink doesn't stop there. He's got a skull on top of one hand, flanked by dark red roses with a thick coil of thorn-tipped vines that twist a tangled path across his forearm. On his other hand is a catholic rosary—a piece I witnessed him get inked into his skin our senior year of high school. It's that one that he's staring at right now. Almost like he's sending up a prayer to Mother Mary.

I don't believe in all of that higher power and praying to the saints bullshit anymore. I stopped long before Carlos died. But if it gives him peace—I roll my shoulders—then who am I to judge?

Jameia stops in front of him, her expression reluctant. But everyone in this room knows why she's here. May as well get it over with.

"Julio," she says softly, "Coach wants to see you."

Julio's jaw tightens, his fingers flexing against his knees as he takes a deep breath. But he doesn't argue. He just nods, disappointment settling in his features as he pushes off the bench and rises to his feet.

Jameia steps back, giving him space to move around her as he heads for Coach's office. Without another word, she falls into step behind him.

"I wouldn't want to be on the receiving end of that conversation," Felix says, sliding onto the bench beside me.

I grimace. "None of us would." Julio failed to lead the team today. But with any luck, Coach won't be too hard on him. He'll get a dressing down for sure, but it doesn't need to be some big thing.

Atticus and Deacon make their way over to us, Deacon's eyes following Julio and Jameia's retreating forms. "You guys ready to head out?" he asks.

I open my mouth to tell him to go ahead without me when Felix chimes in, "I've got it. You three get out of here. I'll stick around and make sure everything's good with J."

My brows pull together, and I'm about to argue when Felix adds, "Your girl is waiting for you, and if I'm not mistaken, there were a couple of other familiar faces in the stands today. Go. I've got it."

twenty-eight

GABRIEL

THE SECOND I step out of the locker room, I'm surrounded by people. First to approach is Cecilia, her arms wrapping around my waist like a lifeline, her cheek pressing against my chest.

"I'm sorry you lost," she whispers, her voice soft but steady.

I tighten my arms around her, holding on just a little longer than I need to. "All good," I reply, though the words feel hollow. What I don't say—what I can't say out loud—is how we just threw away our shot at the NCAA selection committee even glancing our way. We would've needed a perfect record for that, and today's loss? It shattered that possibility. I force out a breath, reminding myself to let it go. Shit happens. Today just wasn't our day.

Pulling back, my hands find Cecilia's waist as I look down at her. Her eyes search mine like she's trying to read me, but I'm too tired, too disappointed, to let her in right now. I kiss the top of her head and glance up, spotting my dad standing a few feet away.

He told me he'd come, but I hadn't been sure if he'd actually show. Didn't want to get my hopes up. But there he is, looking a little out of place amongst the college crowd in his dark blue Levi jeans and button-down shirt, but he's here all the same.

His eyes light up when they meet mine, and he strides over, clapping a hand on my shoulder.

"Gabriel," he starts, his accent more pronounced than usual as a grin stretches across his face. "Your speed out there? Maldita sea, hijo." —*Damn, son.*— "Como una bala." —*Like a bullet.*— "And that goal ..." He pauses, shaking his head in awe. "I haven't felt this alive in years, watching you play like that."

I nod, trying to let his praise sink in, but it feels like it's floating just out of reach. "Thanks, Pops. I appreciate you coming." It's too bad I couldn't have shown him a win.

"I wouldn't have missed it," he says, his chest puffing out a little. "Can't wait to see you on the field again."

He gives me a quick pat on the back before stepping away, and as soon as he does, I see Asher and Adam lingering nearby. They approach with the same awkward energy they always carry, especially Adam, who looks unsure if he should even be here.

"We didn't know if we should stick around after the game," Adam starts, his voice a little hesitant. "But, uh, I just wanted to say—you were great out there, man. This was my first soccer match, and, damn ..." He rubs the back of his neck. "I didn't realize how savage you guys could get."

"Yeah," Asher chimes in, giving me a nod. "You killed it, bro. You guys play almost as dirty on the field as we do on the ice." He chuckles. "We still on for the gym later this week?"

I smirk, appreciating the compliment. "Yeah, we're still on. Thanks for coming, guys."

"Of course," Asher says, a small smile on his face. "We'll catch you later, then."

They give me a final nod before turning to leave. My dad offers a quick goodbye too, telling me once again how proud he is, and then it's just Cecilia and me. Atticus and Deacon pass by us, both of them looking exhausted but in decent spirits.

"We're heading out for a drink," Atticus calls over his shoulder. "You coming?"

"Nah," I shake my head, "I'll catch you guys later at the house. You both played a good game."

They wave me off and head out, leaving the two of us in the growing quiet. I glance back down at Cecilia, her hand still loosely gripping mine.

"Where'd Adriana go?" I ask, my eyes scanning the parking lot one last time.

Cecilia gives me an apologetic look. "I might have convinced her and Kenji to leave before the game ended," she tells me. "Julio kept looking out at the stands during the game. I think she was the reason he was out of sorts today, and I wasn't sure if her sticking around would make things worse between them." She shrugs. "Thought it was best to play it safe."

I nod, the tension of the day still coiling in my chest. "Yeah, good call."

We walk in silence across the parking lot to her white Jeep Wrangler. I toss my bag into the backseat, the thud of it punctuating the quiet. The drive starts the same way—quiet, Cecilia's hands gripping the wheel, and my mind replaying every single moment of the match, every mistake, every missed opportunity.

I can't stop thinking about our loss, so I look for a distraction. "What's the plan on Monday?"

The question hangs in the air, and I can see Cecilia tense up beside me. She knows what I'm asking, knows Monday is the day Austin gets sentenced. "What time do I need to be ready?" I add, trying to make the question as casual as I can.

She exhales slowly, her grip on the steering wheel tightening. "I ... I've been meaning to talk to you about that," she says, and I don't miss the apprehensive tone in her voice.

"I ... uh." She swallows hard before clearing her throat. "I was thinking maybe you'd sit Monday out."

Her statement hits me harder than I expect it to. "What?" I glance at her, trying to get a read on her face. "Why would I do that?"

Cecilia worries her bottom lip. "It's not a big deal," she tells me, though whether she's trying to convince me or herself, I'm not entirely sure. "It's just that Mr. Ayala will be there. Along with my parents, too. I just ... I think it's better if I take care of this on my own." She can't be serious right now. "Besides, you have classes that day, and we don't know how long we'll be in court. It could wind up being an all day thing, and you have practice you'll need to be at."

It's not the words themselves—it's the way she says them, like she's keeping me at arm's length. Hurt flares deep in my chest. And despite my efforts, my next words come out sharp and edged with anger. "You don't want me there."

She lets out a breath, one that screams frustration. Her fingers flex around the steering wheel. "It's not like that."

"Sure as hell feels like that, Cecilia."

Her lips press into a tight line, and the rest of the drive to my place is thick with tension. When we finally pull up, I'm still simmering. As soon as we step out of the Jeep, I can't help but confront her.

"I don't get why you don't want me there," I say, my voice louder than I intend. "It's like as soon as shit is good between us we're right back on the hamster wheel and you're shutting me out of your life again."

Cecilia slams her door and steps around the SUV to face me. "You're blowing this way out of proportion," she tells me.

"I don't think I am," I snap. "But explain it to me, then. Huh? If it's not a big deal, explain why you don't want me there?"

"It's not that simple. I just don't want you getting dragged into—"

"I'm already in this, Cecilia!" My hands are shaking, and I rake a frustrated hand through my hair. "Why are you acting like me being there for you is a sudden inconvenience?"

"I'm not," she snaps, her voice rising to match mine. "But this isn't about you."

I take a step back, her words slamming into me, and suddenly, I feel like I'm losing more than just the argument. Shaking my head, I force myself to take a steadying breath. Now isn't the time. I just lost my game. I'm pissed about that. About the NCAA bullshit. And now she tells me this. I'm not in a good head space to have this conversation.

"Fine," I mutter. "You do you." I'll let it go for now but we sure as hell are picking this conversation back up tomorrow. "I'm going to make us some food. I'm fucking beat."

I walk toward the porch, but when I realize she isn't following me, I turn around. "You coming?"

Cecilia bites her lip before shaking her head. "I, um ... I actually have to go."

"What? Why?" I ask, unable to hide the confusion in my voice. I watch her closely, waiting for her to look at me, to give me some sort of hint into what she's thinking, but Cecilia refuses to meet my gaze.

She hesitates, just for a second, then says, "I promised my mom I'd help her tonight. She's um, making arrangements for one of those dinner things my dad's always hosting for work." Her words come out too fast, and the smile on her face feels forced.

And she still isn't looking at me.

She's lying, and I know it. All of her usual tells are right there—the way she avoids my gaze. How she fidgets, wringing her hands together. I can even hear it in the way her voice goes up a notch at the end of her sentence. She's a terrible liar, and it drives me insane that she thinks I'm stupid enough to fall for it. I don't know what's going on with her right now, and I don't have the energy to push her for answers.

Not tonight. Not when I know it'll only lead to a fight.

Whatever is swirling in that pretty little head of hers, it's making her too guarded to be honest with me. Maybe even too guarded to be honest with herself. Fuck if I know. I don't want to leave shit like this but I know better than to push Cecilia when her walls go up like this.

"Whatever," I mutter, turning away, my chest tight with frustration. I force myself to climb the last of the porch steps before heading inside, not waiting for her response. The door clicks shut behind me with a soft snick, the sound louder in the silence it leaves behind.

I stand just inside the entryway. My back pressing against the solid wood of the door until I hear the sound of her engine roar back to life. With a sigh, I shake my head. Disappointment weighs heavy across my shoulders as I head for the kitchen, but as soon as I open the fridge, my appetite disappears and I find myself slamming the door.

"Fuck." Breathing heavy, I hang my head. I hate giving her space. I hate when she shuts down and pushes me away like this.

Tomorrow. I remind myself. Right now, I just need to drag myself upstairs to my bed and get some sleep. We'll talk and figure all of our shit out tomorrow.

twenty-nine
CECILIA

"YOU SHOULD PROBABLY ANSWER HIM," Adriana says, flopping down on the bed beside me. She hands me my phone, her eyes narrowed with curiosity. Her fingers tapping against her bedspread in a restless rhythm.

A quick glance at the screen shows Gabriel's name flashing across it. I silence the call, the sound disappearing as I set the phone on the bedspread beside me. "I'll call him back later." My pulse drums louder than it should.

Adriana scowls up at me. "What's going on with you two?"

"Nothing." The word tastes sour. I lean back against the pillows, trying to shrug it off. "I'm just not in the mood to talk. Besides, I'm here visiting you right now." I nudge her with my foot, hoping to divert her attention. "It's not a big deal."

She doesn't buy it. Not even a little. "Bullshit." She throws a pillow at me, dead-on aim, her eyes accusing me of lying. "What am I missing?"

I sigh, grabbing the pillow and hugging it to my chest. "Nothing. I just—" I hesitate, biting down on my bottom lip. I don't really know how to explain it. "After the game, things got ... weird."

"Weird how?" Adriana pushes, sitting up straighter now, all her attention on me.

I hesitate, the words sticking in my throat. The pit in my stomach from this morning hasn't gone away. It's only gotten heavier. "I told him not to come to court on Monday. For the sentencing."

Adriana's confusion deepens, her brows pulling together. "Why would you tell him not to come? He's been with you through everything, Cecilia. I thought you'd *want* him there."

I close my eyes, letting out a frustrated breath. "I know," I say, my voice barely above a whisper, "It's not that I don't want Gabriel to be there. It's just ... I don't know what to expect. I haven't seen Austin since the arrest, and just thinking about him and the others makes me want to crawl out of my skin. It's like all of a sudden, I can't breathe," I confess. " And I'm doing good now—*we're* doing good—but what if I fall apart when I walk into that courtroom? I don't want Gabriel to watch me break down again."

"Cecilia." Her voice is steady, but there's an edge to it. She's not letting me off easy. "You don't know how you'll react. You might be fine."

"No." I shake my head, pressing the heel of my hand to my chest, trying to ease the tightness. "I won't be. It's Austin, Adriana. I'll lose it. I know I will." I've been building this up in my head ever since Mr. Ayala gave me the date, and no matter which way I look at it, I'm not going to be okay. "And Gabriel—he finally sees me as strong, as someone who's capable. Not some broken thing in need of saving. I can't let him see me weak again. Not when we've come this far."

Adriana stares at me for a beat, her fingers twisting around the loose thread of her shirt. She's silent, but the weight of her gaze is enough to make me squirm.

"I don't get it," she says. "You guys are doing great. Solid, even."

"That's exactly my point," I whisper, opening my eyes to look at her. "We've worked so hard to get here. In the beginning, it was like he was always walking on eggshells. We both were. But now, he treats me like an equal. Not some sad, broken little thing in need of fixing. I can't risk falling apart in front of him. When I see Austin, Parker, and Gregory ... if I have a panic attack or just ... break, it'll remind him of that girl he first met. The one who was so broken and lifeless and bloodied on the locker room floor." I rub my thumb over the scars on my wrists. The ones I don't bother hiding anymore. "It'll remind him that I'm someone in need of saving."

Adriana's lips part as if to say something, but she stops, her brow furrowed in thought.

"Cecilia," she starts, her voice soft but firm, "I get why you'd feel that way, I do. But ..." She shifts, sitting up straighter, her hands gripping the edge of the bed now. "You're not the only one with damage." She shakes her head, her dark hair shifting with the motion. "He's not going to see you as weak because you struggle. He knows how strong you are. And honestly, pushing him away when he's trying to be there for you? It's cruel."

Her words sting, sharp and undeniable, like a slap to the face. My breath hitches, guilt surging like a wave. "I'm not trying to push him away," I admit, my voice small. "I just ... I'm scared, Adriana. I don't want him to look at me like I'm broken again."

She reaches out, her hand covering mine. "Do you love him?" she asks me.

The question hits me hard. I blink at her, caught off guard. "What?"

"Love," she says. "Do you love him? You don't need to answer that question. Not for me. But I think you need to decide for yourself whether or not you love him. And if you do, then figure out if you can accept his love in return. Because being there for you, Cecilia, that's how Gabriel shows you he loves you. Taking care of you and protecting you. Keeping you out of harm's way. He does that for you because nobody ever did it for him. The people who've claimed to love him the most are the ones who carved his deepest wounds. Can you let him love you the way he needs to? Or will you break his heart all over again by refusing to let him love you in the way that is his?"

I inhale sharply. "Loving me is one thing. But I can't be protected twenty-four-seven. Not from living life itself."

Adriana nods. Her expression thoughtful. "I wasn't there when Carlos died," she tells me. "I'd already fucked up by then so I wasn't in their friend group at the time. But I saw what he was like in the wake of it all. The empty, hollow shell."

My heart hurts thinking of what it must have been like, losing his twin like that. It's hard to think of Gabriel as a shell of himself when the Gabriel I see now is so vibrant and full of life.

"I wasn't there when his parents got divorced either," she tells me. "Or when his mom started taking the pictures of his brother and then of him down from her walls. We weren't friends when his mom stopped looking at him. Or when his Dad started spending more time in the office or at a bar than he did at home."

Her smile is soft and sad. "Alejandra didn't leave by choice. But she left nonetheless. In the thick of Gabriel's world falling apart when at the time, she was probably the only person he'd have accepted comfort from."

I don't ask how she knows about all of that. Adriana's known Gabriel and the others since they were kids. And honestly, I don't really care how she knows, because her words dump a bucket of ice-cold water over my head and make me instantly realize my mistake as I piece together the losses Adriana lays out for me.

His twin brother commits suicide.

His mother openly rejects him.

His father loses himself to alcohol and his grief.

One of his best friends moves away.

In such a short span of time, Gabriel lost so much.

Some by choice and others not, but still, the effect is all the same.

And now, here I am, doing very much the same. By protecting myself, I'm pushing him away. Rejecting him in a similar manner to that of everyone else who came before. I'm hurting Gabriel. I didn't think about how much he's already lost. How much it probably costs him every time he opens up, every time he fights for me, for us, knowing how easily rejection can come.

Oh my god. Last night ... What did I do?

"You're right," I murmur, squeezing her hand back. "You're so right. I can't—" my breath seizes in my lungs. "I was selfish. I'll fix this. I'll—" I can't finish the sentence. My chest is so tight. Gabriel had been forced into the role of protector. He was our very own Guardian Angel. I always thought of him as strong. Untouchable. But I never stopped to look at the flip side.

Abandonment.

No wonder Gabriel held on so tight.

No wonder he wanted to fix all of my problems. To protect me and make sure I was always okay.

No wonder he wanted to save me.

Because nobody bothered to save him when he needed saving.

Adriana's smile is soft. "It's hard to see the hurt when someone is so good at hiding it," she tells me. "And Gabriel's had a lot of practice."

"I'm going to fix this," I tell her.

She nods, though her eyes still hold that familiar weight. "I know," she tells me. "Because you love him."

A ghost of a smile plays over my lips. "Yeah. I really do."

"Damn straight," she says with a playful shove. Then, she leans back, eyes on the ceiling. "You two are good together."

Despite everything, I laugh, the tension easing just a little. "Thanks, Adriana."

"Anytime," she says, her lips quirking up into a smirk. "Now, seriously, go home and call your man back before he blows up your phone again. You know he's not gonna let it go."

I pick up my phone, glancing at Gabriel's missed call with a new sense of clarity. She's right. He won't let it go—because he cares. Because he loves me. And I need to show him I feel the same, that I trust him with all of me, the good and the broken.

thirty
CECILIA

I PULL up to Gabriel's house, a knot tightening in my chest. This conversation can't wait, but my hands still shake as I knock on the door. The seconds drag, my stomach churning as I try to figure out how to fix this mess. When the door finally swings open, it's not Gabriel standing there.

It's Felix, his broad grin quickly shifting into a frown when he sees my face. "Hey, what's up?" he greets, leaning casually against the doorframe. "Gabe's not here."

My heart sinks. "Do you know where he went?" I ask, my voice tight.

"No clue. I thought he was with you." Felix offers me a sympathetic shrug. "Wanna come in and wait? I'm sure he'll be back soon."

I hesitate, but the last thing I want to do right now is sit in Gabriel's house, drowning in my own thoughts. "That's okay. I'll just head home and give him a call later."

Felix watches me for a moment, concern flashing in his dark eyes, but he nods and steps back. "Alright. I'll let him know you stopped by, yeah?"

I give him a weak smile, turning back toward my Jeep. My head's spinning. My thoughts are all over the place and my gut is screaming at me to call Gabriel. But I don't. Some things ... they just need to be said face-to-face.

The drive back home feels longer than it should. My mind replays the argument we had last night, over and over. Each time, my chest tightens a little more. What if he's done with me? What if I pushed him too far this time?

I pull into the driveway, and my heart skips a beat. Gabriel's here, sitting on my porch steps, his elbows on his knees, his head hanging low like the weight of the world rests on his shoulders.

I freeze for a second before quickly turning off the ignition. He looks ... wrecked. Haggard, like he hasn't slept.

This isn't how I pictured our conversation starting. I had this whole plan. I'd apologize. I'd tell him I was wrong and that I want him to come to the sentencing with me. But now, seeing him like this, so worn down ... I don't know where to begin.

Gabriel lifts his head as I step out of the Jeep, his red, bloodshot eyes locking onto mine. My heart stutters, guilt twisting inside me like a knife.

"Hey," I give him a small wave, approaching him with slow and measured steps.

Gabriel's jaw is tight when he looks at me. Slowly, he pushes to his feet. "I can't do this shit anymore." His voice is rough, and his words slice through me like a blade. My breath catches in my throat. *He's breaking up with me.* The thought is like a punch to the gut. My eyes sting with unshed tears, but I force them back.

Now isn't the time to fall apart.

"I'm sorry," I whisper, my voice barely audible.

He shakes his head, frustration tightening his features. "I called you six times, Cecilia. Six."

I flinch. The guilt digs in deeper, hollowing me out. "I—"

He cuts me off, his voice rising with every word. "I knew you needed space last night, so I gave it to you. But today? I called you, and you didn't answer. I show up here, and your parents say you're not home. That you left early and didn't tell them where you were going." His voice cracks, pain etched across his face. Frustration bleeds through his every word.

The anguish in his eyes makes my chest tighten. I open my mouth, but nothing comes out. There's nothing I can say to make this right.

"Do you remember what happened the last time I couldn't get a hold of you?" Gabriel's tone hardens, his jaw clenching. "Do you remember how sick with worry I was when you went missing?"

Tears prick the back of my eyes, my chest squeezing tighter, but I swallow them down. My feet shuffle back, a small retreat.

Gabriel's frustration snaps, "Do you have any idea what's been running through my head all day? Every fucked-up possibility. Every goddamn nightmare I've tried to push away. You could've been hurt, taken again by Holt's fucked up family ... or worse."

His words cut deep, and I start to shrink into myself, folding in like I can somehow hide from the weight of his anger, the intensity of his pain.

But my reaction only makes things worse.

"Don't do that," he snaps, stepping forward, his voice raw. "Don't act like you're afraid of me when you know ... you fucking *know* I would never hurt you."

"I'm sorry," I mumble again, but it sounds hollow. Like a reflex.

Gabriel groans, raking his hands through his hair. He paces the small space in front of the porch. Agitation vibrates off him, his shoulders tight with barely contained frustration.

"Fight with me!" His voice thunders through the air, startling me.

I freeze, staring at him. I don't recognize this version of Gabriel. I've never seen him like this. Never this ... I don't even know.

He spins on his heel, hands in his hair, and curses under his breath. "Fuck. I need you to fight with me, Cecilia. When things get hard, when it's uncomfortable—don't shut me out. Don't just ... disappear. Fucking fight."

I blink, struggling to keep up. "I don't— What are you talking about?"

Gabriel's chest heaves with each breath, his eyes wild with emotion. He steps toward me, then stops, like he can't trust himself to get any closer. "You pull away when things get tough, and I ... I can't do that anymore."

"I don't pull away," I whisper, but even as the words leave my mouth, I know they're not entirely true.

"Yes, you do," he says, his voice softer now, but no less intense. "You retreat into yourself. You shut me out. And I ... I fucked up with the wedding. I know that. But this?" He gestures between us. "This won't work if we keep running from each other."

Tears pool in my eyes, blurring my vision. "I don't know how to fix it," I admit, my voice breaking. "I'm not trying to push you away. I went to your house before I came home," I tell him. "I was going to talk to you. To apologize. I know how we left things last night was not okay, and I wanted to fix it."

His expression softens, his frustration bleeding into something else. "We fight, baby. We fight together. When it gets hard, we push through. I need you to trust me. To know that no matter what, I'm here."

His words crack something open inside me. It's like I've been holding my breath, and now, finally, I can exhale.

Gabriel steps closer, his hand reaching out to brush a tear from my cheek. "You're safe with me, Cecilia. You always will be."

I close my eyes, leaning into his touch, letting his warmth pull me back from the edge.

"I know," I whisper, my voice thick with emotion. "I'm sorry. I want you to come with me tomorrow. I want you to be there."

Gabriel's arms wrap around me, pulling me against his chest, and I sink into him, letting his presence calm some of the anxious energy thrumming through me.

"There was never any doubt in my mind that I'd be going with you," he tells me.

I pull back just enough to stare into his honey-brown eyes, "Really?"

Gabriel presses his lips to my temple and takes a deep breath. "Of course, baby. I'm always going to be by your side," he murmurs against my hair. "Always."

I sniff, my fingers digging into his skin. "I thought you were breaking up with me," I confess.

Gabriel draws back, his face visibly stricken. "What—"

I bury my face against his chest. Hiding, I know. But I won't be able to get the words out if I look at him right now.

"I went to Adriana's today and we talked," I tell him. "She was there when you called and she saw me ignore it. So ... she uh ... she kind of set me straight."

"She did?"

"MmHmm." I reach up and wind my arms around his neck. Gabriel walks me back with him until the backs of his feet meet the porch steps. He drops onto the step, tugging me down with him. He positions me in his lap. My legs straddling his hips. One of his hands moves to behind my knee, the other holds me firm around the waist.

"And how exactly did Adriana manage that?" he asks. I snuggle deeper into his embrace. I like when he holds me like this.

"She reminded me of something really important," I tell him. Taking a deep breath, I lift my head because what I'm about to say next is the kind of thing you need to look in a person's eyes for.

"Oh yeah?"

Biting my lip, I nod.

"And what was that?"

Taking a deep breath, I go for broke. "She reminded me of the fact that I love you."

Gabriel freezes. His lips part, and his eyes grow wide. "Me?" he stammers. "You love me?"

His fingers flex around me, and I nod my head, a stupid grin tugging at the corners of my mouth. "Yeah," I whisper the words softly. "I love you."

His entire face softens. "You mean it?" he asks, almost like he can't believe the words.

"Yes!" I tell him. "You challenge me. You make me feel cherished and safe. You are so different from me in so many ways, and that terrifies me sometimes. But you make me feel loved, and you make me want to live. And not just for you, but for me too. You bring out the very best parts of me, and I want to be that," I tell him. "I want to be the best version of myself, and I am when I'm with you."

"Baby." That one word is said with so much reverence.

"You are something else, Gabriel Herrera. And I think I'd very much like to spend my future with you."

His eyes are tender as he runs the backs of his knuckles along my face. "I love you," he says and my heart expands in my chest. "And baby, I'm never breaking up with you. Don't ever let your head wander in that direction, okay?"

I nod, my eyes suddenly filling with happy tears.

"I gave you space last night because I knew you needed it. But first thing this morning, I was here to get you." His hands run down my sides to settle on my waist. "I was upset because I was worried about you," he tells me. "You not being here, not knowing where you were or if you were okay, I don't want to feel panic like that ever again."

"I'm sorry," I tell him. "You won't."

He nods, his smile curling the corners of his mouth. "I know," he tells me. "Because you love me. And now that I know that, I'm never letting you go."

Laughter bubbles up inside of me. "Is that so?"

Gabriel nods before leaning forward to capture my mouth with his. I sigh into his kiss, his tongue sweeping against mine. "I love you," he tells me between kisses. "I love you so fucking much."

"I know," I tell him, nipping playfully at his bottom lip. "You show me every single day."

thirty-one

CECILIA

GABRIEL and I barely speak the entire ride back from court. The car hums with the weight of what just happened, the silence between us thick but not uncomfortable. It's over. It's really, finally, over.

I can feel Gabriel checking on me in the small, unspoken ways he always does. His hand stays wrapped around mine on the drive, his thumb tracing soft circles over my skin, grounding me when my mind wants to spiral.

He brought me coffee this morning, sat with me through the entire sentencing, never once letting go. And now ... now we're going home.

It's surreal. All of it. The weight I've been carrying for what feels like forever, it's ... not gone necessarily. I'm not sure it'll ever truly go away. But it's no longer this heavy oppressive thing dragging me down.

Gabriel pulls into the driveway, cutting the engine before turning to face me. His honey-brown eyes are filled with that familiar concern, but they're softer now, like he knows what's going on inside my head. I'm so grateful for him.

"You ready to go inside?" he asks, his voice gentle.

I nod, my throat too tight to speak. The last thing I want right now is to be alone, but the thought of going home to my parents hovering over me didn't sound appealing so we came here, to Gabriel's.

We step out of the car and make our way to his front door. It's weird, the normalcy of it all, walking back into his house after everything that went down today. The sentencing went quicker than I expected, but it didn't make it any less emotionally draining. Seeing Austin, Parker, and Gregory again—it brought back all the fear and the trauma, but it was different this time. Gabriel was right there, holding me through every second of it.

Something settled inside of me as each one of them entered their plea of guilty. I know they weren't confessing to what they did to me last summer. But it was vindication nonetheless. They hurt me. They admitted it in court. And now it's on the record. They can't take it back.

I follow Gabriel inside, kicking off my shoes by the door but then I hear a chorus of "SURPRISE!"

My head jerks up to find Felix, Julio, Deacon, Atticus, and Adriana just past the entryway. There are balloons all over the place. Felix is holding a cake. And hanging above the staircase is a hand-painted banner that says "Congrats on Putting out the Trash."

"You guys—" a watery smile spreads across my face.

"We didn't want you to be sad," Adriana says.

"Yeah," Felix chimes in, stepping forward to show me the cake. "Today is a day to celebrate. Those fuckers got what they deserved, and we're going to par-tay!"

"Did you know about this?" I ask, nudging Gabriel with my elbow.

He shakes his head. "Nope. But I'm not surprised." He shifts behind me, wrapping his arms around my waist. I lean into his embrace.

"Oh, yeah?" I ask, tilting my chin up to look at him. "Why's that?"

Gabriel shrugs. "It's what family does."

"Come on! J made food," Atticus chimes in, leading our group into the kitchen where we find a spread of carne asada, tortillas, rice, and beans.

My vision blurs. "You guys didn't need to do all of this," I tell them.

Gabriel presses a kiss to the side of my neck.

"Yes, we did," Julio tells me, an almost apologetic smile on his face. "You're one of us," he says. "And we take care of our own." My heart melts into a puddle. Not so long ago, Julio was the one telling me to let Gabriel go, and now, to have his acceptance ... I don't know. To belong— I can't help but grin.

Gabriel grabs a couple of water bottles from the fridge, but his gaze is locked on me, watching my every move. There's this unspoken understanding between us, like he knows what I need before I even have to ask.

I take a sip of the water he hands me, feeling it cool the

previous tension in my chest. For a while, we just stand there as everyone else grabs plates and moves about the room.

"Bro, did you ask her yet?" Felix asks.

"I'm getting there," Gabriel growls at him.

My brows furrow. "Ask me what?"

"Well, get on with it," Atticus adds, then we can really celebrate.

"What are they talking about?"

Gabriel shakes his head. "Ignore them," he tells me. "They're meddling."

Deacon steps up beside me and offers me a plate. "We're meddling because you're taking your sweet ass time. Stop being a pussy and ask her already."

My curiosity is officially peaked, and I give Gabriel a look that says, *well?*

He chuckles before leaning forward to capture my lips. The kiss is quick, gentle, but it still does something to my insides and has me leaning into him, desperate for more.

"Move in with me," he murmurs against my lips.

His words cut through my desire, and I freeze, my breath hitching as I look up at him. For a second, I'm not sure if I heard him right.

"What?" My voice is barely a whisper, my heart pounding so hard I swear he can hear it.

Gabriel steps closer, his hands slipping around my waist, pulling me against his chest. His forehead drops to mine, and I feel his exhale, the warm rush of his breath brushing over my skin.

"Move in with me," he repeats, softer this time, his voice rough around the edges. "I know it's fast, but I don't care. I want you with me, Cecilia. Every day."

My mind spins, trying to process the weight of his words. Move in with him? Live here, together? I look around the room at all of the waiting faces. "You guys are all cool with that?" I ask.

I'm greeted by a chorus of "Yes!"

"I ... I don't know what to say," I murmur, my voice trembling.

Gabriel tightens his grip on me, his hands trailing up to cup my face. "We all talked about it over the weekend," he tells me. "You don't have to decide right now. Just ... don't say no. Okay? Think about it."

He kisses my temple, his lips lingering there for a second longer than usual, and it's like the world stops spinning. His touch, the warmth of his breath on my skin—it anchors me in a way that nothing else ever has. I want to move in with him. I'm ready to be all in.

"Yes."

The word slips out before I can even think it through, but the second I say it, I know it's the right decision. His head jerks back, his eyes wide, searching mine like he's trying to make sure he didn't imagine it.

"What did you just say?" His voice is hoarse, his hands trembling slightly where they rest on my cheeks.

I smile, the weight of everything lifting off my chest. "Yes, Gabriel. I'll move in with you."

"Woohoo!" Felix cheers. "We've got ourselves a new roomie, boys!"

A slow grin spreads across Gabriel's face, and before I can say anything else, his lips crash against mine. The kiss is hungry, desperate, and full of relief, like he's been holding his breath waiting for me to say those words. His hands slide down my body, gripping my hips as he pulls me closer, and I can't help the soft moan that escapes me.

"We'll see you guys later," Gabriel says between frantic kisses.

Everyone laughs and cheers and tells us to get our asses upstairs. So we do.

Within seconds, we're stumbling toward the stairs, our lips never breaking contact. Every inch of me is on fire, my body aching for him. By the time we reach his bedroom—our bedroom—my shirt is halfway off, and Gabriel's hands are roaming over my bare skin, leaving a trail of heat in their wake.

"I love you," he groans against my lips as he lifts me, my legs wrapping around his waist. The strength of his arms holding me steady makes me feel weightless, like nothing in the world can touch me as long as I'm with him.

"I love you, too," I breathe, my voice barely audible over the sound of my racing heart.

Gabriel carries me to the bed, his hands never leaving my body, his lips trailing down my neck, over my collarbone, and lower. Every touch, every kiss feels like a promise. We're together. We're solid. We've been through hell, but we're still standing. And this—us—it's the one thing I know I can always count on.

As we come together, everything else fades away. There's only him, only us, and the overwhelming certainty that this is exactly where I'm supposed to be.

We're endgame. Always.

julio

. . . .

"ALRIGHT, FUCK IT," Felix announces suddenly, hopping down from the counter with a sharp thud. His gold chain catches the late afternoon light, glinting as he strides toward the fridge. The kitchen is already filled with the lingering scent of frosting and sugar, a reminder of the untouched cake waiting for us. "Since Cecilia's upstairs with Gabriel, I say we dive into her celebration cake now. She's not gonna miss it, and I'm starving."

Deacon grins, pushing off the sink where he's been lazily leaning. His hazel eyes light up with that usual mischievous glint. "Seconded," he says, cracking his tattooed knuckles like he's ready to dig in.

"Thirded," Atticus chimes in, already reaching for the stack of plates on the counter. His white-blond hair flops over his forehead as he moves around the room.

I stand back, watching as they pull out the cake with more excitement than grown men should have for dessert. The sound of the knife slicing through the layers of cake fills the air, along with the soft clink of forks being handed out. The smell of buttercream frosting thickens the atmosphere, making my stomach growl, but I can't bring myself to move.

It's low-key ridiculous, but maybe also exactly what I need right now—a distraction. Something to focus on that isn't her. I lean against the wall, arms crossed, my eyes drifting—no, *pulled*—to the far side of the kitchen. Adriana sits there, perched at the table, phone in hand. She's been quiet most of the afternoon, more focused on her screen than any of us, like we don't even exist. Every few minutes, her lips curl into a smile, the kind that makes my gut twist like a knife.

Felix is happily passing out cake slices when Adriana finally looks up, her brow furrowed in that irritated-but-curious way she does when we're about to do something stupid. "Are you guys seriously eating her cake without her?"

Felix shrugs, handing Deacon a large slice, the frosting thick and white, almost too perfect to touch. "She won't mind. We'll save her a piece. Or, you know, we'll apologize later. It's easier to ask for forgiveness, right?" He grins, and Deacon chuckles as they dig in.

Adriana rolls her eyes, but there's a small smirk playing on her lips as she looks back down at her phone. It's the same smirk that used to drive me insane—when she'd tease me, push me, waiting to see how far I'd let her go before I snapped. But now? Now, that smile, those little games, they're not for me anymore.

Everyone's in good spirits. Happy. Relaxed. You can feel it in the air, the sense of relief after everything that went down in court today. Everyone except me.

I catch the way her fingers fly across the screen, the way her thumb pauses, then she smiles again—*probably texting Kenji.* And fuck, I don't know why it bothers me. It shouldn't. But there's something about seeing her smile at her phone, knowing it's not meant for me, that sets me on edge.

I shouldn't care.

I don't care.

Goddammit.

Felix elbows me, jolting me out of my thoughts. "You're awfully quiet, man. This is supposed to be a party. You good?"

I grunt, more of a reflex than an actual response. I cross my arms tighter over my chest, my fingers digging into my sides. Felix doesn't let it go, though. He tilts his head, giving me that look that says he knows exactly what's going on inside my head.

Pretty sure you don't, cabrón.

"Go talk to her," Felix says, nodding toward Adriana, his voice low but insistent. "Smooth things over. You've been weird all day."

"I'm not being weird," I mutter, shifting my weight from one foot to the other, my boots scraping softly against the tile floor. My hands itch to do something—anything—but I shove them deep into my pockets instead, trying to shake off the restlessness that's been gnawing at me since I saw her smiling at that damn phone.

Felix raises an eyebrow, not buying it for a second. "Yeah, you are. And it's pretty obvious why."

Across the kitchen, Adriana lets out a soft laugh at something on her phone, the sound cutting through the easy vibe of the room and settling right in my chest like a weight.

"It's fine," I grind out the words.

Felix follows my gaze and smirks.

"Right. Sure, bro. Keep telling yourself that."

Atticus slides off the counter, his wide grin in place as he joins in. "Come on, Julio. What's the deal between you two, anyway? You've been eyeing her all afternoon like she's gonna vanish or something. And don't think I didn't notice that shit at the barbeque. That was ... intense." He pops a piece of cake into his mouth, waiting for my reaction.

I roll my eyes, but it's weak, half-assed. I can't even muster the energy to pretend it doesn't get to me. "There's no deal," I say, my voice rough. "We're just ..."

The words stick in my throat, refusing to come out. I don't know what we are. We're ... not friends. Definitely not friends. And god knows I don't want to be her friend. My voice drops, and the frustration seeps through. "Shit is complicated. Okay?"

"Complicated, huh?" Deacon joins in, leaning back against the counter, cracking open a beer with one swift motion. "Sounds like a load of bullshit, man."

"Agreed," Felix laughs, stuffing another bite of cake into his mouth.

"Fuck you," I mutter, snatching the beer out of Deacon's hand before he can take a sip.

"Hey!"

"You're underage," I remind him.

Atticus snickers, "Sucks to be you."

"You're not twenty-one yet either," Deacon grumbles, but the corners of his mouth lift.

"Fucking freshman," Felix teases, taking the beer from me and taking a long sip. The tension in the room cracks a little with the banter, but it's still there, hovering just beneath the surface.

Felix leans back against the fridge, wiping his mouth with the back of his hand. "So, you guys excited about having a chick in the house? I know we all told Gabe it was cool, but let's be real —having Cecilia move in? That's gonna be a big fucking adjustment."

Atticus shrugs, a wide grin spreading across his face as he grabs another forkful of cake. "Having her here is gonna be interesting, but Cecilia's cool. Plus, it'll be nice to have someone live here who actually picks up after themselves for once."

Deacon nods in agreement. "It'll be different. Like, she's not just any girl. She's Gabriel's girl. That changes the dynamic."

Atticus grins, tossing an arm around Deacon's shoulder, pulling him close. "We handled your needy ass just fine when you moved in. Cecilia will be a piece of cake compared to you, bro."

"Fuck off," Deacon says, shoving him off, though his smile never falters. "Not the same, man. I'm just saying, it'll be ... different."

The room fills with the sound of laughter and light-hearted teasing, the mood lifting around me. But my focus keeps drifting back to Adriana. She's still smiling at her phone, completely tuned out from everything happening around her.

Felix nudges me again, this time softer, his eyes scanning my face like he's trying to read my thoughts.

"Talk to her," he says, voice low but firm. "Or you're just gonna let this shit fester."

I shake my head, a cold knot forming in my stomach. "It's not that simple."

"Then make it simple," Felix shrugs, taking another bite of cake like this isn't slowly killing me from the inside out. "You're the one letting it hang in the air, man. That's why it feels weird."

I glance at Adriana again, my chest tightening, the weight of all the unsaid shit between us pressing down hard. She glances up briefly, catching my eye, but it's only for a split second. Just long enough to make my pulse spike before she looks back down, her smile fading like she never even saw me.

Maybe Felix is right. Maybe I'm just letting this thing between us twist into something bigger. Something messier than they need to be.

But when I look at her, all I feel is ... *complicated.*

And I have no idea how to untangle it.

———

Up next we'll be heading back to Sun Valley. Go back to where it all started and you might just see a few of our favorite Boys of Richland, too. *cough cough * It's Julio. You'll definitely catch a glimpse of Julio. https://amzn.to/4eVUkBy

For more from the Boys of Richland, be sure to add the next book in the series to your Goodreads TBR: https://

www.goodreads.com/book/show/220834011-t-s   We'll   be
kicking off book 4 with a new couple. Any guess at who it
might be?

As always. Thank you so much for reading! If you'd
take a moment to leave a review on your favorite retailer of
choice, I would really appreciate it! xoxo

about the author

Daniela Romero is a USA Today and Wall Street Journal bestselling author. She write steamy, new-adult and paranormal romance that delivers an emotional roller coaster sure to take your breath away.

Her books feature a diverse cast of characters with rich and vibrant cultures in an effort to effectively portray the world we all live in. One that is so beautifully colorful.

Daniela is a Bay Area native though she currently lives in Washington State with her sarcastic husband and their three tiny terrors.

In her free time, Daniela enjoys frequent naps, binge reading her favorite romance books, and is known to crochet while watching television because her ADHD brain can never do just one thing at a time.

Stop by her website to find all the fun and unique ways you can stalk her. And while you're there you can check out some free bonus scenes from your favorite books, learn about her Patreon, order signed copies of her books, and swoon over her gorgeous alternative cover editions.

www.daniela-romero.com

You can join my newsletter by visiting
https://hi.switchy.io/VIP